NORTHUMBERLAND
NATIONAL PARK

NORTHUMBERLAND
NATIONAL PARK

Tony Hopkins

Webb & Bower

MICHAEL JOSEPH

Acknowledgements
Thanks are due to many people for their help and advice
in the preparation of this book: in particular Tony
Macdonald, Angus Lunn, Douglas Robson, Beryl Charlton,
Jim Parrock, Mick Eyre, Colin Jewitt, Brian Galloway, Ian
Kerr, Stuart Ball, Ian Wallace, Janet Bleay, Terry Carroll,
Eric Dale and Graham Coggins.

Many of the photographs were taken by Eric Dale for
the countryside Commission. Additional photographs
were used with permission of the following: T Carroll
pages 91, 99 (above), 117, 120; B Charlton page 24; Tony
Hopkins pages 10, 15, 17, 21, 33, 37, 41, 42, 50(2), 59, 61,
63, 79, 93, 94(2), 96(2), 97, 98, 99(below), 101, 103, 106,
107, 108(below), 111, 112, 116; A Miller pages 52, 66, 77,
80, 83, 86, 95, 119(below); and the Museum of
Antiquities, Newcastle, pages 23, 53.

First published in Great Britain 1987 by
Webb & Bower (Publishers) Limited
9 Colleton Crescent, Exeter, Devon EX2 4BY
in association with Michael Joseph Limited
27 Wright's Lane, London W8 5SL
and The Countryside Commission,
John Dower House, Crescent Place,
Cheltenham, Glos GL50 3RA

Designed by Ron Pickless

Production by Nick Facer/Rob Kendrew

Illustrations by Rosamund Gendle/Ralph Stobart

Text and new photographs Copyright © The Countryside Commission
Illustrations Copyright © Webb & Bower (Publishers) Ltd

British Library Cataloguing in Publication Data
The National parks of Britain.
Northumberland
1. National parks and reserves — England —
Guide-books   2.   England — Description and
travel — 1971-   — Guide-books.
I. Hopkins, Tony
914.2′04858   SB484.G7.

ISBN 0-86350-132-X

Typeset in Great Britain by Keyspools Ltd., Golborne, Lancs.

Printed and bound in Hong Kong by Mandarin Offset.

Contents

Preface

Northumberland is one of ten national parks which were established in the 1950s. These largely upland and coastal areas represent the finest landscapes in England and Wales and present us all with opportunities to savour breathtaking scenery, to take part in invigorating outdoor activities, to experience rural community life, and most certainly, to relax in peaceful surroundings.

The designation of national parks is the product of those who had the vision, more than fifty years ago, to see that ways were found to ensure that the best of our countryside should be recognized and protected, the way of life therein sustained, and public access for open-air recreation encouraged.

As the government planned Britain's post-war reconstruction, John Dower, architect, rambler and national park enthusiast, was asked to report on how the national park ideal adopted in other countries could work for England and Wales. An important consideration was the ownership of land within the parks. Unlike other countries where large tracts of land are in public ownership, and thus national parks can be owned by the nation, here in Britain most of the land within the national parks was, and still is, privately owned. John Dower's report was published in 1945 and its recommendations accepted. Two years later another report drafted by a committee chaired by Sir Arthur Hobhouse proposed an administrative system for the parks, and this was embodied in the National Parks and Access to the Countryside Act 1949.

This Act set up the National Parks Commission to designate national parks and advise on their administration. In 1968 this became the Countryside Commission but we continue to have national responsibility for our parks which are administered by local government, either through committees of the county councils or independent planning boards.

This guide to the landscape, settlements and natural history of Northumberland National Park is one of a series on all ten parks. As well as helping the visitor appreciate the park and its attractions, the guides outline the achievements and pressures facing the national park authorities today.

Our national parks are a vital asset, and we all have a duty to care for and conserve them. Learning about the parks and their value to us all is a crucial step in creating more awareness of the importance of the national parks so that each of us can play our part in seeing that they are protected for all to enjoy.

Sir Derek Barber
Chairman
Countryside Commission

Introduction

Northumberland was the ninth national park to be designated, in 1956, the year of the Hungarian uprising and the Suez Crisis, when the world seemed close to the edge of darkness. But on dark days we always look to a brighter future. The issues of conservation and access to the countryside, loudly proclaimed in pre- and post-war years, still had resonance in the mid '50s and we were ready to take to the hills. Since then the spiritual currency of the national parks has increased with each passing year. This is particularly true of Northumberland, the least populated and least visited of the ten, ideal for people seeking solitude in a remote landscape.

The hills that dominate the park rise in altitude as they extend northwards, from the Whin Sill and Hadrian's Wall, across the fields and wastes of the North Tyne Valley and Redesdale, to the heather

Mid-winter in the Cheviot hills; the view north east from Windy Gyle.

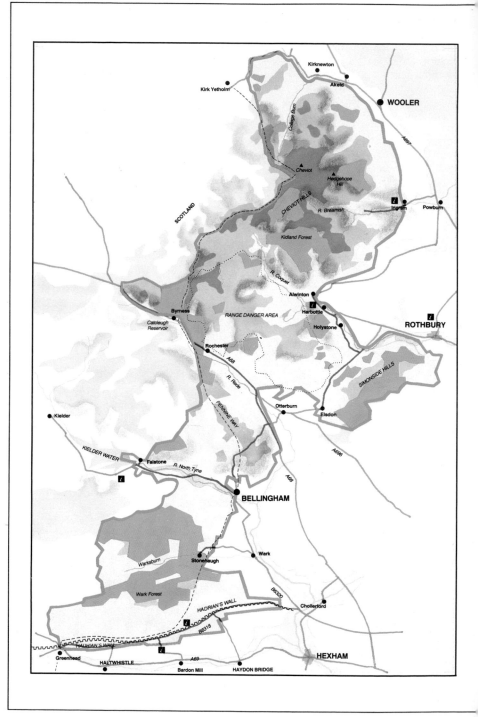

moors of Simonside and the high grassy domes of
the Cheviot massif. Before designation, there was
talk of separating the area into two parks, or of
including the coast and Kielder forest. The present
boundary is a compromise linking the fine scenery
of the Roman wall with the great dome of the
Cheviot.

The climate can be uncompromising; short
springs and windswept summers are considered
normal. But there are days of unrivalled beauty
even in the worst of years, and the autumn, the 'back
end', can be breathtaking.

The particular beauty of Northumberland
National Park lies in its scale, for within an area of
398 square miles it imposes an impression of width
and distance, rolling hills and wide valleys drifting
away to the horizon. Many famous writers have
visited the Border hills but few have captured this
spirit of wilderness. Daniel Defoe was impressed
more by the sweep of history:

> 'Northumberland is a long coasting county . . .
> bounded by the mountains of Stainmore and
> Cheviot on the west, which are in some places
> inaccessible, in many unpassable. Here is
> abundant business for the antiquary: every
> place shews you ruined castles, Roman altars,
> inscriptions, monuments of battles, of heroes
> killed, and armies routed.'

More than 250 years later the park has still yielded
no more than a fraction of its secrets. History is close
to the surface and provides an unusually clear
perspective of our cultural heritage, absorbed into
the busy mix of farming and forestry. And as
patterns of land use have changed, wildlife habitats
have been created or modified and our most elusive
birds and beautiful flowers have found a refuge.

The Northumberland
National Park.

1 Rocks and landform

Fire and water created the Northumberland landscape, moulding the rock upon which the vegetation and soil now rests. The Earth was formed about 4,600 million years ago, a long time for different rocks to be created, shaped and disposed of. If this period were compressed into a single day with the clock now striking midnight, the oldest rocks discovered in Britain would have cooled down at about 9.30 am, and Northumberland's main elements of scenery would have been formed between 9.45 pm and 10.30 pm. The Ice Age, which dramatically altered the shape of the hills and valleys, began at half a minute to midnight and ended a quarter of a second ago.

Six hundred million years ago an ocean covered most of Europe and beneath its surface mud and sand built up to immense depths; eventually the land masses on either side of the ocean moved together. This resulted in the buckling and folding of the sediments and the creation of a vast mountain range across the Highlands of Scotland and North America. Although not so dramatic, there was also some folding across the Southern Uplands and the Borders. In Northumberland the oldest of the folded sediments to be exposed at the surface are of the Silurian period, laid down around 420 million years ago. The best exposures are to be seen at the headwaters of the Rede alongside the A68, and especially near the head of the Cottonshope Burn, and in the Coquet Valley.

As soon as the dust settled on these Caledonian Mountains the process of erosion began. They were gradually eaten away by rivers; mud, sand and pebbles were carried southwards and deposited in extensive lakes, one of which covered the Border area. Subsequent iron staining turned the sediments a deep orange colour. The resulting sedimentary rock, of the Devonian Sandstone period, is exposed today in the cliffs above the Jed Water north of Jedburgh. But the aftermath of the mountain-building phase gave rise to irresistible pressures beneath the crust. There was considerable volcanic

The north gate of Housesteads Roman Fort, with Hadrian's Wall and Sewingshields Crag in the background.

activity, and it is to these violent events of 380 million years ago that the Cheviot Hills owe their existence.

Magma (liquid rock) was forced up through the Silurian strata and reached the surface via a series of circular vents. There were colossal explosions throwing out ash and rock fragments, followed by lava flows which soon covered the whole area of the Cheviots. Today, the rock fragments or pyroclasts form local deposits exposed at such sites as Ravensheugh on Thirl Moor (NT 80–08–) and at Gaisty Burn (NT 78–10–). The volcanic lavas, mainly andesites, cover 350 square miles of the Cheviots, both north west and south east of the Scottish border. They weather easily and their pebbles and boulders form the beds of most of the streams in the watershed. Pink or purple/grey is the usual colour for the andesites, with a white speckling caused by the weathering of felspar in the parent material. The purest 'glassy' andesite is black with fine red veins and is still to be found at such sites as Carshope, in the banks of the River Coquet. Because the andesites are relatively base-rich with only an intermediate silica content, the soils that cover the Cheviots tend to support grassland rather than

The White Land of the Cheviot uplands, between Windyhaugh and Carlcroft.

What Northumberland may have looked like when the Cheviot volcanoes were still active.

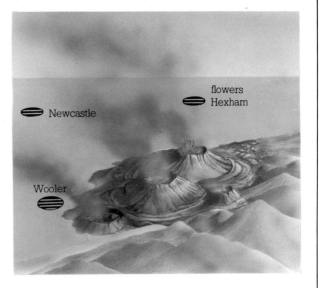

Linhope Spout, where the Linhope Burn cascades down from the granite core of the Cheviot massif.

heather. This adds a pale or frosted quality to the landscape and has earned the grassy plateau one of its most attractive local names, the White Land.

Shortly after the Cheviot volcanoes had fallen silent and their 'extrusive' rocks had cooled, further igneous activity saw the upwelling of a massive 'intrusion' of magma which failed to reach the surface and which cooled very slowly to form granite. This is a silica-rich rock composed of quartz, felspar and mica. Weathering and erosion of the overlying volcanic rocks had exposed the roof of the hard granite core and this now forms the heart of the high hills area, including both Hedgehope (NT 944198) and The Cheviot itself (NT 908205). Exposures of the crystalline rock are few however, the best known being above Linhope Spout (NT 959169), above the Spout at Great Standrop and in Cunyan Crags on the south-east slope of Dunmoor Hill. Where the magma came into contact with andesite it altered the mineral composition of the latter material making it much harder and darker with large crystals of felspar and mica. This metamorphic aureole encircles the Cheviot core and its resistant strata now form most of the rocky tors so characteristic of this area. Housey Crag (NT 957218) and Long Crag on the south side of the Harthope Valley are impressive examples of this 'baked' andesite.

Whilst the granite stock was certainly the most

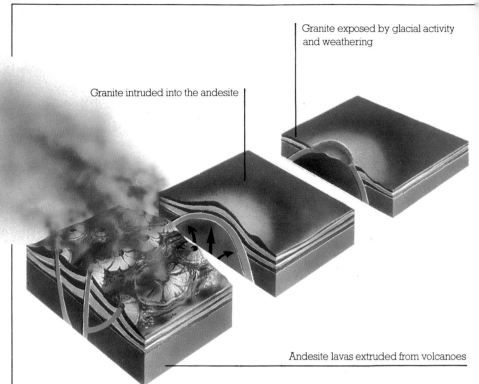

Granite exposed by glacial activity and weathering

Granite intruded into the andesite

Andesite lavas extruded from volcanoes

important product of upthrusts of magma into existing sedimentary and igneous rock it was by no means alone, for it was followed by minor intrusions through fissures in the andesite and even in the granite itself. These intrusions or 'dykes' are composed of either felsite or porphyrite, often salmon-pink in colour, the former a fine-grained material similar in chemical composition to granite, the latter more like andesite. North of Harden and Biddlestone, on the hillside above Coquetdale, is a site where the porphyrite welled out between existing strata and formed a blister-shaped structure called a laccolith (NT 958087). This proved to be the ideal situation for a quarry, and for many years the attractive 'red whin' has been extracted as a roadstone fit to grace the Mall in London. It is also used on the sides of virtually every motorway, its red colour helping to distinguish the hard shoulder from the main driving lanes.

About 350 million years ago the Upper Old Red Sandstone period gave way to the Carboniferous.

Cross-section of granite with andesite and baked tors.

This was heralded in Northumberland by the laying down of sediments eroded from the extinct volcanoes, transforming the Cheviot Hills into an island surrounded by shallow seas. Pebbles accumulated into banks and ridges, exposed today as conglomerate at such places as Roddam Dene (NU 02–20–) and at Windy Rigg on the Border, below Windy Gyle, whilst sand and mud – layer

The Biddlestone/Harden quarry, where porphyrite ('red whin') is extracted for roadstone.

upon layer as the sea ebbed and flowed – were flushed out into wide deltas. Every now and then these must have cleared sufficiently for tiny shellfish to flourish. Thus the layers of sandstone and shale are now interleaved with thin bands of Limestone derived from the shells. This sequence of deposits is known as the Cementstone Group and its finest exposure is along the 150 ft (45 m) high gorge of the Coquet Valley above Alwinton (NT 90–06–).

Soon after this, across what is now the North Sea and north-west Europe, a much bigger river system developed which began to unload even greater amounts of sand on top of the Cementstone deposits to the south and east of the Cheviots. This river must have been several times as impressive as anything found in Britain today, and the constant strong current allowed no fine muds of lime-secreting organisms to interrupt the deposition of fine sand. There were continuous currents which caused cross-bedding throughout these sediments and the sand gradually accumulated, on a subsiding floor, to a thickness of about 1,000 ft (305 m). The topography at that time must have been very dramatic, the Cheviots as yet much higher and unaffected by glaciers, the river delta stretching out for miles as it

An exposure of cementstone along the Coquetdale Gorge, at Barrow Scar.

pushed further and further into the sea. Today this Fell Sandstone forms a wide arc of high crags and scarp slopes facing inwards across the fertile lowlands of the Cementstone deposits and towards the Cheviots. In the national park the imposing heather moors of the Simonside (NY 02–98–) and Harbottle Hills (NT 92–04–) are typical examples of this important landscape feature.

Eventually, sequences of mud and lime were laid down on top of the Fell Sandstone, indicating that the great river must have diminished in power and even dried up at times. Marshy ground appearing above sea level would have been colonized by primitive plants. Peat was formed from their dead but undecayed leaves and stems, to be covered in turn by fresh deposits from the re-awakened river. This oft-repeated sequence of sandstone-shale-limestone-coal forms the Scremerston Coal Group, named after a village near Berwick. Drift mines have exploited the thicker seams in Redesdale and along the North Tyne Valley, as at Plashetts and Lewisburn at Kielderwater.

The next major sedimentary episode, this time of national significance, was the laying down of Carboniferous Limestone. In Yorkshire and Derbyshire this phase saw the creation of what were to become the key elements of the landscape, pure deposits of limestone topped by Millstone Grit, but in Northumberland the seas were coastal and the deposits were therefore of shale and sandstone with much thinner bands of limestone. Only in the south of the national park are there any limestone outcrops (though they occur in the sediments east of the park boundary), and these are both impure and localized. Coal seams laid down towards the end of the Carboniferous period were of much greater importance to Northumberland for they brought prosperity to the landowners and employment to the population. But nothing of these Coal Measures occurs within the national park.

It is to earth movement at the very end of the hot, swampy Carboniferous period that we owe another important phase in the building of the landscape. First, the Cheviot massif was pushed up and tilted slightly eastwards. Second, a series of faults and subsequent erosion created the valleys that now radiate out from the heart of the Cheviots; the College, Harthope and Breamish Valleys all owe their existence to these Armorican earthquakes. Finally, magma was again pushed up through fractures in the Earth's crust. The latter occurred

The Harthope Valley, following a fault line north east from the heart of the Cheviots. In the distance are the two highest hills, Hedgehope (left) and the Cheviot (right).

295 million years ago and resulted in the formation of the Whin Sill, one of the most famous landscape features in northern England. The magma was intruded between existing sediments rather like hot jam being squeezed into the layers of a sandwich cake. To the north, on what is now the Northumberland coast, it found its way into Fell Sandstone strata to form the Farne Islands and the hills or 'heughs' on which the castles at Dunstanburgh and Bamburgh were built. To the south the magma pushed between Carboniferous Limestone strata, and subsequent erosion exposed it as a dramatic ridge running for many miles across the national park and beyond the Cumbrian border. The dip slope, capped by grassland, sweeps south whilst the scarp, a near vertical wall of shadowy rock, faces north. The Romans used the crest of the ridge for their wall, anticipating the sobering effect it might have on Caledonian troublemakers.

The Whin Sill and its associated dykes are composed of a very hard dark grey rock called quartz-dolerite, and several quarries once extracted whin-chips for roadstone. Two of these, at Cawfields (NY 714667) and at Walltown (NY 67–66–), offer interesting cross-sections of the sill but reveal

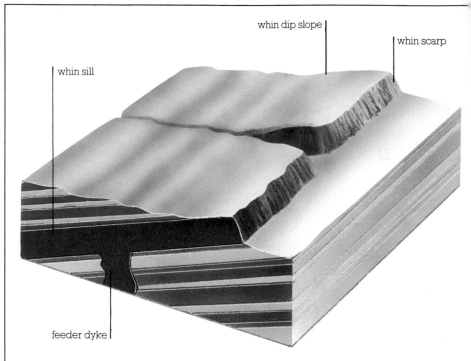

The dip and scarp slope of the Whin Sill. Magma was pushed upwards and outwards between the existing sediments nearly 300 million years ago.

a lamentable lack of planning control prior to the designation of the park.

After this burst of earth shattering and building the north of England settled down to a relatively quiet period which extended throughout the Mesozoic era. Even the creation of the Alps about thirty million years ago caused only minor ripples. This was the period of great igneous activity in the Brito-Icelandic region, with outpourings of lava (including those of the Giant's Causeway) and dyke swarms centred on the island of Mull, of which the local representative is the Acklington dyke.

The rivers that now lattice the county of Northumberland evolved in this long quiet phase. Most of those on the English side of the Cheviots flowed north east to join the Tweed, whilst the rivers draining the central and southern sections of the park, the Aln, Coquet, Wansbeck, Blyth and Tyne, all flowed east to the sea. It is possible that the North Tyne cut off other headwaters and captured the Rede and the present upper reaches of the North Tyne, both of which had once fed the Wansbeck, and the Warksburn which had originally flowed into the Blyth.

For many millions of years forest and fens must

The River Coquet, looking north towards the Cheviot hills.

have blanketed the ground between the rivers, but this came to a chilly end about two million years ago when the climate gradually deteriorated and summer after summer failed to melt the snow accumulating on the hills. Soon Britain was in the grip of an Ice Age and all the vegetation and soil vanished as if it had never been. There were numerous respites as temperatures improved to previous levels, but each time a cold glacial phase intervened to wipe the landscape clean. The most recent of the glacial episodes, called the Devensian, was at its most severe about 18,000 years ago. Huge ice sheets pushed eastwards from southern Scotland and the Lake District, meeting smaller ice streams generated in the Cheviots and on Carter Fell. The movement and sheer weight of ice and debris chiselled into the existing valleys and changed their shape. Pebbles and boulders were wrenched loose and carried inexorably eastwards until, somewhere just beyond the present coastline, the banks of ice came up against an even more massive body of Scandinavian ice and were deflected south. By the time the climate had at last improved and the ice had melted, silt and stones had been lodged all over the lowlands and in the hill valleys. Pebbles from

Scree, known locally as 'glidders', on the steep slopes of Brough Law above the Breamish Valley.

Galloway littered the Coquet and others from the Tweed Valley were piled above the North Sea shore. Rubble and mud was everywhere. Boulder clay or 'till' as this glacially derived material is known, covers most of south and east Northumberland to a depth of up to 25 ft (7.5 m).

Although the major landscape features were able to withstand the glaciers there were many changes of detail. Curious 'meltwater channels' appeared, having been formed beneath the ice as gravel-laden water bored its way through ice and rock. These dry channels can be seen today at such places as Langlee (NT 96–23–) in the Harthope Valley and below Yeavering Bell (NT 92–29–) and Humbleton Hill (NT 96–28–) near Akeld. They are steep-sided and often start and end abruptly. The main A697 road from Newcastle to Coldstream makes use of one of these meltwater channels at the village of Powburn (NU 06–16–). Drumlins, large oval mounds of boulder clay grouped together in a 'basket-of-eggs' formation, were deposited and moulded by the moving ice sheets; together with 'kames' and 'kettleholes' they can be seen in the valley south-east of Wooler. In the uplands severe freezing and thawing shattered rocks and caused cascades of scree to build up on the steeper valley-sides. These banks of unstable scree survive to this day and are known locally as 'glidders' – dangerous places for unwary walkers.

The retreat of the ice was probably complete 13,000 years ago, but so far as the vegetation was concerned the climate was still distinctly arctic. There was even a regression which allowed small glaciers to reappear in the Cheviots; the Henhole and Bizzle valleys (NT 88–20– and 89–22–) developed cirques as a result of this.

With the weight of the ice removed, the north of England slowly began to raise itself to its previous height. Rivers cut deeper channels to carry away meltwater, and as a result some of the most beautiful gorges and white-water torrents were created. The mineral-rich soils, evolved from rocks ground up by the ice, were soon colonized by tundra plants and the countryside began to resemble Lapland or Siberia. Not comfortable or recognizably rural, but well on the way to recovery.

The presence of a broad 'land bridge' between Britain and the Continent allowed shrubs and trees to spread northwards as the arctic conditions waned. About 10,000 years ago most of Northumberland would have been covered by a quilt of grassy heathland with shrubs such as dwarf birch, willow and juniper. These were crowded out by a rapid expansion of hairy birch which dominated the main 'pioneer' woodland for over 1,000 years. Pine grew on the drier hillsides and hazel came to dominate the lowlands of Northumberland, but birch was still the characteristic tree all over highland Britain. Norway spruce, which had been an important part of our interglacial flora, seems to have been unable to take advantage of the milder climate. Oak and wych elm, then alder and lime, tracked their way further and further north. The climate changed again, this time becoming warm and wet allowing broad-leaved forest trees to flourish as never before. Alder was able to colonize the hillsides and river banks and is still to be found as relict woodland in several remote places such as the upper Harthope Valley (NT 94–21–).

Britain became an island about 7,500 years ago, calling a halt to possible late additions to the fauna and flora. But for a further 1,500 years the climate still favoured rich deciduous woodland, and temperatures were a degree or so higher than they are today. Early colonists such as dwarf birch and juniper managed to survive through this Atlantic period in only a very few places; the former is still found at one site on a moor above the North Tyne Valley, the latter at several localities including Holystone Burn (NT 94–01–). Along with the warmth of the Atlantic period there was a great deal of rain, however, and this meant that peat began to form on plateaux and hilltops. The demise of the primeval forest had begun.

Alder still survives as a dominant tree in post-glacial relict woodland.

2 Prehistory and early settlers

The virgin forests of Stone Age Northumberland may have resembled a Garden of Eden, but for a very long time they did not attract our ancestors. Early hunters who followed herds of red deer and aurochs (wild cattle) across the marshy plain from western Europe kept to the lowlands. As the North Sea basin filled with water about 8,000 years ago these nomadic Mesolithic people established seasonal camps along the new coastline and up the wider valleys, where natural clearings were more plentiful and communication and access easier. Several sites for flint 'microliths', cores, blades and scrapers, have been discovered on the ridges of Fell Sandstone that surround the Cheviots, but so far little evidence of Mesolithic activity has been found along the upper valleys within the national park.

The population must have grown over the years with the improving climate until the holding capacity of the land was reached. The 'hunter-gatherers' were not entirely dependent on taking things as they found them however, and it is likely that they set fire to sections of forest to promote flushes of foliage for animals to browse. It is even possible that they shepherded or herded wild animals, a significant step towards domestication. But their way of life made no lasting impression on the landscape.

Agriculture, involving the growing of cereals and the husbanding of sheep and goats, began in Britain with the arrival of Neolithic settlers about 6,000 years ago. Because of the requirement for open land their first task was to clear the 'wildwood', and the resulting change in vegetation is faithfully recorded in the layers of pollen grains preserved in the peat of marshes and mires. In the northern hills the first sign of a decrease in tree pollen and an increase in characteristic 'open-ground' plants such as ribwort plantain begins about 4,000 years ago, very late compared with the rest of the country. Settlements seem to have been associated with valleys and lowlands, in such areas as Coquetdale and the lower Breamish Valley rather than in the Cheviot uplands. The farmers from across the sea brought a new ethos to the countryside but for many years the hunter-gatherers continued to follow their traditional life-style in the wilder uplands and there may have been little competition between the cultures. What happened to the wandering people in the end is a mystery, though a process of adaptation and absorption seems the most likely result of continuing contact.

Neolithic stone axes, often derived from the Langdale quarries in the Lake District, have been discovered in scattered sites below the 500 ft (152 m) contour. On the Northumberland coast at Dunstanburgh, a prehistoric site for the exploitation of quartz-dolerite (hard volcanic 'whinstone') has recently been discovered but most of the axes made of this material post-date the Neolithic period.

The most dramatic and enduring features left by the Neolithic inhabitants of Britain are associated with death and religion rather than with their social or working lives. The excavation of earthen long barrows in the south of England has revealed not only a complex funerary tradition at this time but also hinted at the belief in an earth goddess who watched over the dead. In the north the equivalent of the earthen barrows are the long cairns, elongated mounds of stone or boulders containing simple rectangular mortuary structures. None of the handful of long cairns found in Northumberland has been excavated in the last fifty years and they can only be interpreted by comparing them with similar monuments elsewhere in the British Isles. Two long cairns overlook Redesdale, at Bellshiel Law (NT 813011) and Dour Hill (NT 792021). Neither is visually very impressive; the Bellshiel Law structure is over 120 yd (110 m) long and 4 ft (1.2 m) high. It has been partly excavated by archaeologists and much disturbed by treasure seekers. Bellshiel lies within the military training area and the Dour Hill cairn has disappeared under a forest plantation, so access to these monuments is not easy.

Until quite recently only one Neolithic site, a farming settlement at Thirlings, near Wooler (NT 956322), was known in the Cheviot area, but in 1979 a long cairn was discovered on Dod Hill above Ilderton (NT 987207). Again this is not a particularly dramatic structure, about 26 yd (24 m) long and up to 5 ft (1.5 m) high, but it represents an important link between the farmers of the late Stone Age and the early metal-working communities that were to flourish for the following thousand years.

The Bronze Age is much better represented in

Bronze Age barbed and tanged flint arrowheads from Northumberland.

Northumberland than the Neolithic. A dramatic increase in the settlement of the uplands, beginning between 3,700 and 3,900 years ago, corresponded with climatic improvement and with the spread of new cultures and technology from the Rhineland. One of these innovations was the knowledge of how to smelt ore and produce the alloy bronze by mixing copper and tin. Durable, keen-edged tools and weapons were the result, but such implements were comparatively rare and quite valuable – hence the continuing use of stone and flint axes by the hill farmers. Early burials sometimes contained a bronze knife or jet buttons, presumably a sign of prestige or to be of some use on the journey to the next life. Bronze Age burials are to be found throughout the central and northern hills of the national park and many graves have been excavated. Most are quite small, often no more than a few yards across, with a low, round cairn of boulders overlying a rectangular stone-lined cell or cist. Inside the cramped chamber the body (one per cist) was contracted into the foetal position and a beaker or food-vessel was placed close by with ritual provisions for the journey. Cists were usually capped with heavy slabs intended to keep the

A Bronze Age cist burial on Dour Hill in Redesdale.

structure secure, but over the years it is the capstones that have proved the undoing of many of them. Farmers are not sympathetic to buried boulders at plough-depth and have been responsible for their removal as inconvenient obstacles or their recycling as useful stone gate-posts.

Many Bronze Age burial sites were robbed long ago by treasure hunters, and sometimes all that is left is a circular scatter of boulders and slabs or even the open cist itself. This can add to the excitement and mystery of a place, particularly when it is wild and remote. Lordenshaws (NZ 05–99–), high above Rothbury and in the shadow of the dour Simonside ridge, is just such a place and has other archaeological attractions too. One of the best sites in the Cheviots is to be found near the top of Knock Hill (NT 99–17–) where there are the remains of three cairns, and another three can be found on Thirl Moor (NT 805084) above Redesdale. An open cist, long robbed of its contents, lies at the foot of Tod Law (NY 900955) and close to a group of small cairns.

Monoliths and henges, inexorably linked with the romance of prehistory, usually date back to the early Bronze Age. Exactly what they were for remains a mystery, which is perhaps one of the main reasons why they have retained their romance, but they could well have served a religious purpose. Recent investigations have shown that they were very carefully set out. Nothing on the scale of Stonehenge was built in the north, and nothing like Arbor Low (in the Peak District) or Castlerigg (in the Lake District) survives in Northumberland National Park, but there are several smaller circles of standing stones to catch the imagination. Aerial photography, which has brought great advances in our understanding of Bronze Age settlements everywhere, has recently revealed the site of a wooden henge monument on the Milfield Plain north of Wooler. Unfortunately, timber-built structures quickly rot away and their previous presence can only be detected by crop marks on agricultural land. Nothing is visible on the ground. In the nearby Cheviots, a site along Threestone Burn near Ilderton (NT 971205) bears the most dramatic surviving stone circle in the park. The name is probably a diminutive of 'Thirteenstone' Burn, since the circle contains thirteen stones of which five remain standing. Elsewhere in the Cheviots, monoliths or single standing stones are to be found at several

places including Humbleton Hill (The Battlestone, NT 969295, which is supposed to mark the site of the battle of Humbleton in 1402) and at Biddlestone (NT 957081). Further south there are interesting groups of standing stones at Dues Hill near Harbottle ('The Five Kings', NT 958001) and at Cawfields next to Hadrian's Wall ('The Mare and Foal', NY 726663), and the remains of a stone circle near Wark on the North Tyne (The Goatstones, NY 831748).

The other tantalizing mystery associated with large boulders and stones on the Northumberland moors, whether capstones, monoliths or the natural debris of glaciation, is that many of them bear complex carvings picked on to their surface about 3,500 years ago. These 'cup and ring' marks, usually involving cup-shaped depressions surrounded by concentric circles and joined to each other by ducts or grooves, have attracted a great deal of attention by modern mystics believing in earth magic. Certainly to come across a carved rock on a lonely hill or moor fires the imagination. Were they maps, fertility symbols, coded messages? Nobody knows. Even the distribution of stone carvings is enigmatic. They are common in the Border Country, fairly

The Mare and Foal, standing stones near Shield on the Wall.

numerous in Yorkshire, local in Cumbria, but very rare throughout the Midlands and the south of England. In Northumberland virtually all the carvings are on soft Fell Sandstone, presumably because of the nature of the stone and the limited scope of masonry tools in the early Bronze Age. The moors of Fowberry and Weetwood, Chatton and Bewick, between Wooler and the coast, contain some of the finest carvings, but there are good examples in the national park at Lordenshaws (NZ 052991) and at Tod Crags (NY 972891).

Standing stones, cists and rock carvings represent the spiritual side of life in the northern hills, but there was a more prosaic side, the day-to-day winning of a living from the land. The Cheviot Hills have provided the majority of clues to land use at this time; the reason is not that the area was intensively farmed, for there is every indication that settlements were widely scattered, but that the thin soils have not been so extensively ploughed subsequently and thus a surface record has survived to this day.

The first clearance of scrub birch from the foothills must have revealed a landscape of stones. Early farmers occupied a good deal of their time (or

Cup and ring marks, carved on to outcrops of Fell Sandstone in the early Bronze Age, are to be seen in several places in the national park. This is one of the easiest sites to visit, at Lordenshaws near Rothbury. In the distance are the Simonside hills.

perhaps the time of their children) collecting up
boulders and stones and dumping them in piles so
that areas of open ground could be cultivated.
These 'clearance cairns', grouped together in
'cairnfields', can still be seen in many places and
are often situated close to signs of early Bronze Age
settlement. Only in the last few years has the extent
of these early settlements been realized or properly
interpreted. It seems that people lived in small
family groups, in huts without any surrounding
enclosure, and would have grown cereal crops and
kept a few domestic animals and stock. Ninety
'unenclosed settlements' have been identified in
Northumberland, the great majority skirting the
lower hills of the Cheviots between the 700 ft (213 m)
and 1,250 ft (381 m) contours. Many of the
settlements had simple field systems attached, but
the fields were usually less than half an acre in size
and the boundaries can only have been
rudimentary, such as a series of clearance cairns or
a low bank. Signs of unenclosed settlements can be
seen (just!) at such sites as Standrop Rigg, Ingram
(NT 951174) and Hazeltonrig (NT 961118). Not
surprisingly it has taken some time to glean
evidence for what may appear to have been an
ephemeral or very simple way of life. However,
aerial photography, fieldwalking and
reinterpretation of old boundaries, excavation and
pollen analysis have all helped to piece together a
system that actually survived for many centuries.
Why and when it came to an end is obscure.

The climate, a degree or two warmer than it is at
present, began to deteriorate about 3,200 years ago,
and it got progressively colder and wetter
(evolving from the 'Sub-Boreal' to the 'Sub-Atlantic'
period) until cereals could no longer be grown on
the higher ground. This may have caused social
stress and a complete change of life-style and
people may have left the hills. Alternatively it is
possible that they stayed but were forced to adopt a
more pastoral economy based on stock rearing. The
first archaeological evidence for change comes with
the arrival of a completely new type of settlement,
dating from about 2,800 years ago. Circular wooden
houses were still the basis of the settlement but now
their number had increased and up to thirty-five
were enclosed within a solid timber stockade, thus
constituting a village rather than an informal family
community. These 'palisaded settlements' were
located widely over much of England but surviving
field evidence, the hollows and grass-covered

An artist's impression of
the palisaded settlement
on High Knowes, Alnham.

mounds that reveal where ditches and ramparts
once stood, is restricted to the Northumberland
hills. Such sites as High Knowes (NT 971125),
Hoseden Linn, Alwinton (NT 918081) and Kidlandlee
Dene, Alwinton (NT 914089), are therefore of special
significance to archaeologists, though the general
visitor may find them disappointing because they
are not readily discernible in the landscape.

There had been little technological advance
through the Bronze Age, no major leap forward to
affect the lives of ordinary people. However, the
arrival in southern Britain of the Celts, from the Low
Countries, provided a new impetus and must have
brought about fundamental changes in existing
communities. The introduction of iron at this time
was also decisive; copper and bronze weapons
were inferior to tempered iron in the hands of
warriors. Whether there was any large-scale
conflict in such an out of the way place as
Northumberland is open to question, but there is no
doubt that social stresses of some sort led to the
palisaded enclosures being replaced by true
defensive settlements with stone ramparts. This
happened around 2,600 years ago. Excavation of
sites has revealed no sudden switch from one to the
other, rather the continuous occupation of hill
settlements with gradual evolution from semi-
defensive palisades to 'univallate' (single rampart
and ditch) and ultimately 'multivallate' systems of
defences.

There were over 150 of these Iron Age hillforts or
defended settlements in Northumberland. Who the
ramparts were intended to keep out is difficult to
say. Possibly neighbouring communities or

wandering marauders intent on stealing stock. Although the internal dimensions of the hillforts were quite small, usually no more than an acre and no larger than those of the palisaded settlements they replaced, the outer rings of the ramparts must have presented a daunting prospect to any aggressor. Even now, almost levelled, they dominate some of the valleys in the national park and provoke several questions, such as how long did it take to raise the ramparts, and why did they need such immense defences? Two of the best hillforts to visit are at Lordenshaws in the Simonside hills (NZ 054993) and Brough Law in the Breamish Valley (NT 998164), but there are many other fine examples. The most extensive settlement of this period is on Yeavering Bell (NT 928293), the broad twin-peaked summit of one of the rolling hills outlying the main Cheviot massif. Here a stone rampart encircles an area of thirteen acres with the 'pock marks' of 130 circular houses. By the standards of its day this was an unusually large community, along the lines of Eildon Hill North in Roxburgh or Traprain Law in East Lothian, tribal centres of the Votadini people.

The rampart and ditch of Harehaugh Iron Age hillfort, overlooking the River Coquet.

3 Romans and the military background

An uneventful life had been a worthwhile aspiration for Iron Age inhabitants of the northern hills. Compared with the quickfire developments in the lowlands, progress had been very steady; Northumberland was a backwater feeling the pull of prevailing currents but never in the mainstream of events. This changed abruptly with the Roman invasion. An empire based on military brilliance was quick to assess the north through a soldier's eye, to appreciate its tactical value and turn it into a borderland – a role that Northumberland has been obliged to play ever since.

Julius Caesar led expeditions across the English Channel in 55 and 54 BC, but there were higher priorities for the Roman Empire at that time and a full invasion was not attempted until AD 43. By then Claudius was emperor and in need of a victory to bolster his prestige in Rome. Britain must have seemed an attractive proposition, and its conquest brought with it grain, mineral wealth, a ready supply of slaves and conscripts, and a chance to reduce incursions and instability in Gaul. It did not prove to be a very difficult task. Cross-Channel trade had flourished for some years previously and the inhabitants of southern Britain were able to glimpse a standard of living hitherto undreamed of. Some leaders of tribes in the South and West probably felt that they might be more secure under Roman patronage and offered their support to the invasion. So, although there was fierce resistance from the Catuvellauni tribe, the arrival of the Roman legions was not such a shock to the South as it might earlier have been.

Once Claudius had gained his success he left the conquest of Britain to his governor and returned home. There followed a thirty-year period of consolidation in the lowlands with only one major revolt – of the Iceni tribe led by Boudica (Boadicea) – to trouble the pacification programme. But the situation in the uplands was very different. This may have been because of the difficult terrain and the fact that the scattered tribes were less amenable to the ways of Rome. Attempts to come to some sort of understanding with the Brigantes eventually failed and in the early '70s the emperor Vespasian decided to eliminate the tiresome resistance in Rome's most northerly province. He appointed successive governors who had experience of fighting in Wales and the North, and encouraged them by taking a personal interest in their progress to work towards a conclusive victory. Julius Agricola, appointed in AD 78, brought the task closest to completion and within an ace of success.

Agricola was a shrewd and fair-minded governor, if we can believe his biographer and son-in-law Tacitus. He was also a brilliant general ('No fort of his was ever stormed, ever capitulated or was ever abandoned'), and after making short work of the Ordovices in Wales and policing that territory with legionary fortresses at Chester and Caerleon, he turned his undivided attention to the North. In AD 79 the Roman legions pushed through the kingdom of Brigantia which had proved so volatile in the early years of Vespasian's reign. The following year they were in full control of the Tyne–Solway isthmus, and in AD 81 Agricola continued the advance into southern Scotland. As Tacitus recorded, 'Astonished by these movements, the terror-stricken enemy never ventured to harass the army, which however suffered much by the severity of the weather; thus time was obtained for founding castles.'

The network of forts built by Agricola served not only to overwinter the army in relative comfort but also intimidated the opposition. The interlinking network of roads between the forts fragmented the native tribes and enabled the legions to respond quickly to any breath of rebellion. When Agricola reached the Forth–Clyde isthmus and settled down in his winter quarters it was in the knowledge that he was insulated against anything that Britain could bring against him. The most important of the lateral roads built at this time was the Stanegate from Corbridge to Carlisle. These were key military installations and the road was a busy one, defended by wooden forts at Vindolanda and Carvoran. The road was sited along the Tyne–Irthing gap, a ribbon of green separating the Pennines from the Border wastes, and the last convenient crossing place before the Scottish Lowlands.

The long straight road that carried the legions northward from their fortress at York to the wilds of Caledonia is called Dere Street. It crossed the Tyne at Corbridge, adding to the strategic value of

The Stanegate ('stone road') as it runs through the Roman settlement of Corstopitum near Corbridge.

Corstopitum, the supply base and fort built on this site. Once it had regained the high ground on the north shoulder of the valley, Dere Street headed north west across Redesdale where it was defended by marching camps and the fort of Bremenium at High Rochester (pronounced Row-chester). The dramatic scenery of the Tyne–Irthing gap and Redesdale forms the southern section of the national park and many of the Roman remains lie within the park boundary, safe beneath a blanket of grass and heather.

When Vespasian died he was succeeded in turn by his sons Titus and Domitian, both of whom continued to support the campaign against the Caledonians. Agricola moved north again in the summer of AD 84 and won a decisive victory at Mons Graupius, the exact site of which has never been discovered. This was the end of any meaningful resistance. Just before the battle the Caledonian leader Calgacus is recorded by Tacitus as having called on his fighting men for a last desperate attempt to turn the tide: 'We, the last men on earth, the last of the free, have been shielded till today by the very remoteness of the seclusion for which we are famed . . . but today the boundary of

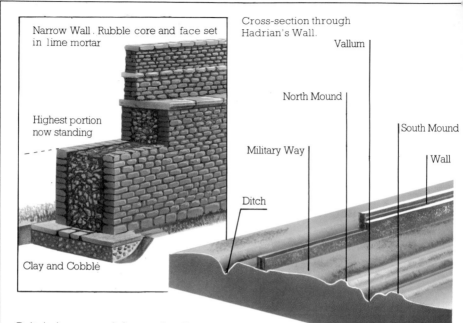

Narrow Wall. Rubble core and face set in lime mortar

Cross-section through Hadrian's Wall.

Vallum

North Mound

South Mound

Highest portion now standing

Military Way

Wall

Ditch

Clay and Cobble

Cross-section showing the main components of Hadrian's frontier: vallum, wall and ditch.

Britain is exposed; beyond us lies no nation, nothing but waves and rocks.'

Immediately after the victory Agricola was recalled to Rome, having served a long term as governor and well pleased with his career in the North. But Domitian and subsequent emperors, including the great warrior Trajan, made no attempt to finish the task in the Highlands. Their interest again lay elsewhere and after only a few years the number of legions based in Britain was cut from four to three, making it virtually impossible for any governor to regain momentum even if total conquest was seen as the only solution. About the year 100 Trajan had his forces withdrawn from the Forth–Clyde isthmus to the Tyne–Solway line, the Stanegate. This time the intention was that the road should serve as a frontier, and a series of small forts at such sites as Haltwhistle Burn and Throp were built to augment the existing forts. Watchtowers were positioned on the ridge of the Whin Sill above the Stanegate, enabling the garrisons to keep in touch with the movements of raiders crossing the scrub and mires to the north.

The Stanegate frontier must have proved an embarrassing failure to those who planned it, for it was quickly replaced. When Trajan died in 117 he was succeeded by Hadrian who adopted a policy of zero growth for the empire. Having acquired first-

Hadrian's Wall, looking
north from Walltown
Crags.

hand experience of the building of turf and timber
barriers in Upper Germany, Hadrian saw the
creation of a wall as the answer to his problems in
Britain. He wasted little time; when he visited the
province in 122 it is possible that the work had
already begun and it is tempting to visualize
Hadrian supervising some of the construction
himself, for he was keen on detail and enjoyed
walking. However, most of the building of the wall
was left to the new governor, Aulus Platorius Nepos.
It was decided to make use of the local sandstone
rather than timber, and numerous quarries were
opened up as the building work moved westward
from Newcastle towards Carlisle. Once across the
River Irthing and into what is now Cumbria, the
barrier was continued in turf. Building in stone was
time consuming; it was imperative to finish the wall
quickly so the army authorities decided to use
traditional materials – earth, turf and timber – on the
western sector and replace them with stone as and
when necessary.

The whole wall-building operation lasted about
eight years, and even as the plan was being
implemented it was altered to take account of new
ideas and experience. To start with, the foundations
of the wall were built to a width of ten Roman feet
(nine and a half English feet or three metres), but
after a while it was decided, again for speed, that a

Turret 35A, at Sewingshields.

width of eight or even six Roman feet was sufficient. This is why there are places today, particularly in the section along the Whin Sill, where a 'narrow' wall can be seen above a 'broad' foundation. More significantly it is obvious that there was some anxiety about the intentions of the Brigantian tribes to the south and the security of the wall system, and about the delay in deploying the Stanegate garrisons to cope with trouble on the north side of the wall. Thus the 'vallum', a ditch with high banks, was excavated south of the wall to mark the rear of the military zone and to control the passage of civilians across the frontier. Instead of relying on a small garrison based on fortlets and turrets and augmented by troops from the Stanegate forts, a whole new series of forts was built into the framework of the wall. These included Brocolitia, Housesteads and Great Chesters on the dramatic central section of the wall running through the national park. Altogether there were twelve forts along the wall between Wallsend (Segedunum) and Carlisle, each garrisoned by 500 or more auxiliary soldiers. In its final manifestation, Hadrian's Wall ran from Wallsend to Bowness, a distance of eighty Roman miles (just over seventy-three English miles). Between the main forts, small milecastles were positioned every Roman mile, and between the milecastles were turrets, two between each

Outcrops of whinstone made the digging of a 'V'-shaped ditch to the north of the wall an extremely laborious business. At Limestone Bank the Romans seem to have given up halfway through.

milecastle. These sheltered the look-outs who probably spent more time fighting cold and boredom than Selgovaean raiders. Given that the army operated in eight-hour shifts, twenty-four troops would be needed daily to man each milecastle and the turrets on either side of it. The total military complement for the whole wall system must have comprised 10,000 men, auxiliary soldiers from all over Europe rather than the Roman legionaries who had actually done the construction work.

Just to the north of the wall was a deep 'v' shaped ditch and bank, a standard Roman fortification, but the vallum to the south only remained in use for a few years and its impact on the landscape today is out of proportion with its value at the time. Over a million cubic yards of stone were used to raise the wall to a height of 16 ft (5 m) at the foot of its ramparts. The whole incredible venture, so costly in time and labour, may have been a device to keep the legions gainfully employed. But whatever his ulterior motives, Hadrian had created the ultimate deterrent of his age and the 'barbarians' were effectively isolated from the empire. For nearly 300 years the wall was the northern frontier of Rome.

Hadrian's successor, Antoninus Pius, moved the frontier further north and ordered a new turf wall to be built across the Forth–Clyde isthmus. To make this defence effective a very large garrison was required; the venture proved uneconomical and the Antonine Wall was abandoned after a few years. Dere Street was still of considerable importance as the main communication route to the North however, and this served to supply a series of outpost forts. These included the refurbished Bremenium at High Rochester and Habitancum (Risingham – pronounced Rizzingham) near West Woodburn.

Forts both north and south of Hadrian's Wall were attacked and demolished in uprisings and skirmishes during the Roman occupation. The wall itself was breached on several occasions too, one of the worst stemming from the withdrawal of much of the garrison by the governor Clodius Albinus while he was trying to maintain a precarious status as 'Caesar' against the emperor Semptimius Severus. Albinus's British army availed him nothing and he died in battle at Lyons in 197. By the time things were back to normal the defences were in a poor state. Severus ordered a rebuilding programme along the whole frontier, including the outpost forts at Risingham and High Rochester between the years 198 and 208. There was considerable unrest in the north still and the rebuilding was not completed without further barbarian attacks. The governor wrote to Severus to this effect, that 'the barbarians had risen and were overrunning the country . . . and that for effective defence either more troops or the presence of the emperor was necessary'.

With the wall system in fighting trim, Severus took up the challenge himself, and Dere Street again resounded to the sound of marching feet. He led a punitive expedition against the Caledonian tribes in 209 and 210, but the old emperor died before he could press home his advantage. His sons, Caracalla and Geta, did not see any profit in continuing the venture and negotiated a peace treaty with the Caledonians before returning to Rome to stake their claims to the empire.

Severus's ill-fated visit to Britain may not have achieved its intended goal but it taught the barbarians a sharp lesson and there was no trouble in the north for another century. Far from being the centre of rebellion, the wall area became a peaceful backwater at a time when the rest of the empire was in turmoil. Gradually the auxiliary soldiers manning the wall forts came to think of Britain as home, to marry local women and to raise their children in the civilian settlements that grew up around the forts.

Hadrian's Wall; the view east from Walltown.

Towards the end of the third century AD there was another bout of political instability caused by the attempts of British governors to use their authority and power to create their own empires. Again there were attacks on the more vulnerable wall forts from native tribes – in particular the Caledonians who had by now joined forces with the Maeatae to form a Pictish nation north of the Forth–Clyde isthmus. The emperor Constantius Chlorus, following in the footsteps of Severus, had the wall and forts rebuilt or repaired and the defences reorganized. He came over to deal with the Picts himself, but followed his predecessor to the grave, dying in York just as Severus had done a century earlier. His actions staved off disaster for some years but strife in the early fourth century culminated in the Barbarian Conspiracy of 367 when there was a well organized invasion on all sides by Picts, Scots, Saxons, Franks and Atocotti. The result was a shattering defeat for the Romans and utter anarchy in the province. The emperor Valentinian sent one of his finest commanders, Count Theodosius, to Britain with a small army to try to regain order. This he eventually achieved, though the frontier was never quite the same. Hadrian's Wall was repaired (it had not been very badly damaged), but the outpost forts were gone and were not replaced.

At the end of the fourth century AD, after a period of uneasy calm, the garrisons were reduced as yet another governor fought unsuccessfully for the imperial throne. By the year 410 the people of the province felt so defenceless against the incessant raids from the north and east that they took matters into their own hands by appealing directly to the emperor Honorius for help. His reply was that they should protect themselves, implying that Rome was no longer in a position to do very much about its outlying possessions. Shortly afterwards, pay and provisions for the troops failed to arrive and Britain was on her own for the first time in 360 years. After such a long presence, the wall garrison by now was inextricably linked with the local community and had probably derived most of its workforce from the resident population, so the end of Roman rule may not have been such a heavy blow after all. Technological and cultural innovation had been absorbed and would stand the people in good stead but the forts and battlegrounds, together with the names Agricola, Hadrian and Severus, drifted into the mists of history.

4 **Roman remains and Celtic farmers**

For many centuries the relics of the Roman frontier were allowed to decay or, worse still, were used as a source for cheap building material. Hadrian's Wall was systematically plundered; most farms and byres within carting distance of the monument were built from its stone, and between 1752 and 1757 General Wade had extensive sections of it levelled and used as the foundations for a road so that troops could be deployed across the country to counter the Jacobite menace. Ironically it is this road, still known as the Military Road, which now furnishes spectacular access to the best surviving relics of the wall.

In past centuries few visitors ever made the long journey north to look at the Roman remains along Dere Street or Hadrian's Wall. Perhaps people were too busy to take a backward glance at their ancestors. It says much for changing attitudes that one of the most famous walkers of the wall, William Hutton, described himself in 1802 as 'perhaps . . . the first man that ever travelled the whole length of this wall, and probably the last that will ever attempt it'.

Hutton was remarkable in that at the age of seventy-eight he walked all the way from Birmingham and wrote a wonderfully eccentric account of his experiences. Travellers today are

Earthworks associated with Hadrian's Wall. To the left is the vallum, to the right the Military Road built in the mid-eighteenth century. At this point east of Brocolitia, the road overlies the levelled remains of Hadrian's Wall.

able to make similar tours in comparative comfort and in a fraction of the time. Two road routes through Northumberland give access to most of the important Roman remains, but wherever possible it is still rewarding to follow the examples of Hadrian and Hutton and go by foot for at least some of the way.

The section of Hadrian's Wall and the Stanegate running from the North Tyne to the Irthing combines the finest Roman monuments with dramatic scenery. Most of this area is within the national park and can be reached conveniently by driving from Hexham northwards on the A6079, then turning west at Brunton on to the B6318, the Military Road, towards Chollerford.

Just before the bridge over the North Tyne is reached, a footpath leads southwards, down some steps and beside a disused railway. This leads to a Roman bridge abutment, an excellent starting place for a tour of the most interesting sites (NY 914701). Nothing of Hadrian's Wall is visible until, half a mile along the path, there is a sharp turn right, down to the river. Here there is a short section of wall 6 ft 4 in (2 m) thick on broad foundations, and nearly 9 ft (2.7 m) tall. This adjoins a guard tower. In Roman

The bridge abutment at Chollerford. Beyond the remains of the guard tower is a short section of Hadrian's Wall.

times the course of the river ran close beneath the tower and the wall was carried over the river on stone piers (the superstructure would have been built of wood). Some time after the wall was built the Romans enlarged the whole bridge system to carry a road; the original abutment can be seen encased in the later structure. The ground floor of the guard tower was used as an undershot water mill and the mill race, covered by massive stone slabs, clips off the projecting spur on which the abutment rests. Perhaps because of the walk involved, the site of the abutment is not heavily visited and has no interpretive information, but it is so unusual and in such an attractive position – shaded by oaks and with a view across the river to the Roman bath-house of Chesters Fort – that it is worth a detour and whets the appetite for the more dramatic Roman ruins to the west.

Back on the road and just after Chollerford bridge the Military Road bears left to the west (take the first exit at the island). A few hundred yards on there is an entrance on the left to the car park of Chesters Roman Fort (NY 913702). Chesters (known to the Romans as 'Cilurnum', meaning 'cauldron pool') lies on much more sheltered ground than any of the other wall forts and the ruins are among the best preserved and most accessible. It was a cavalry fort of five-and-a-half-acres, a third extending northwards beyond the line of the wall to allow for rapid deployment of troops. Only part of the fort is exposed, but this includes a fine headquarters building with an underground strongroom, the commander's house, and all the fort gateways. Towards the river there is a well preserved section of the bath-house with an alcoved changing room and a sophisticated latrine flushed by the cold-room overflow. The museum associated with the fort contains some important carvings and inscriptions, most of which were collected or salvaged in the nineteenth century by John Clayton, a wealthy local landowner and antiquarian.

From Chesters the Military Road leads uphill, through Walwick and out of the soft tree-lined valley. To the right is Black Carts (NY 882714), its section of wall and turret isolated in green pasture, not dramatic but certainly eye-catching. On the crest of the hill the road bears left at Limestone Bank. The small car-parking space on the north side of the road is easily missed but provides one of the few stopping places on this stretch of the Military Road, with an excellent section of the vallum to the

Turret 29A at Black Carts.

south. A gate just next to the parking space gives access to the edge of the Whin Sill (NY 877716) and a view across North Tynedale to Chipchase Castle. Although the wall has not survived (most of it is under the road) there are the remains of the Military Way and a milecastle, and parts of the ditch which at this point cuts its way through solid whinstone. The task of constructing the ditch was never finished – reason prevailed – and it is possible to find massive boulders with wedge-holes cut into the thin quartz veins to allow the whinstone to be split. Like the bridge abutment at Chesters, this part of the wall is full of interesting detail and alive with atmosphere, and is rarely visited compared with the popular fort sites.

Back on the Military Road and a mile further west is a metalled car park for visitors to the Roman fort of Brocolitia at Carrawbrough (NY 861713). The fort remains lie unexposed and although the dimensions of the buried walls look impressive it is difficult to gain any impression of the place. It was built at about the same time as the narrow wall, across the existing vallum, and it must have been a windswept and damp posting for the foot soldiers from south-west Europe who made up the *cohors quingenaria* in the days of Hadrian. The attraction in a visit to Brocolitia lies not in the fort but in the replica of the Mithraic Temple discovered in 1949 a few yards to the south west. The real altar stones and statues of the small temple have been removed to the Museum of Antiquities in Newcastle, but the reconstruction has now weathered into a passable replica. Near to the temple, but not accessible, is a marshy hollow marking the site of Coventina's Well, a shrine which

South of Hadrian's Wall the dip slope of the Whin Sill is much greener and more fertile than the moorland to the north. On the crest of the hill, between the shelterbelts of trees, are the remains of Housesteads Fort.

yielded the most important hoard of Roman coins ever found on the frontier.

From Brocolitia the Military Road leads straight for two miles, then leaves the line of the wall and bears left. A side road to the south, with a small building and telephone kiosk on the corner, offers the only stopping place (NY 816701). To the north, the wall follows the Whin Sill as it gains height to Sewingshields Crags. A walk to the crags (NY 800701), either from further along the wall or along the track a little way to the west, brings you to one of the most impressive viewpoints along the whole whinstone ridge. Stone from the wall was used to build the farm and the tower-house or castle which once stood close by. A local farmer discovered the sleeping court of King Arthur in a cave below the castle, but his courage failed him before he could blow the horn to break the spell. Unfortunately the poor farmer could never quite remember the spot again, so the discovery is unconfirmed . . .

About a mile west of Sewingshields is the best known of all the wall forts, Housesteads (NY 790688). The extensive car park, with its visitor centre, is a few hundred yards from the fort but the ascent along the metalled track allows you to form an impression of the fort's situation on the dip slope of the Whin Sill, and to call in at the small museum housing some of the finds. The need for a fort on this site, to succeed the Stanegate fort of Vindolanda and guard the Knag Burn Gap on the line of the wall, meant that normal theories of design had to be modified by the engineers of the second legion who built the fort. The alignment was east–west rather than

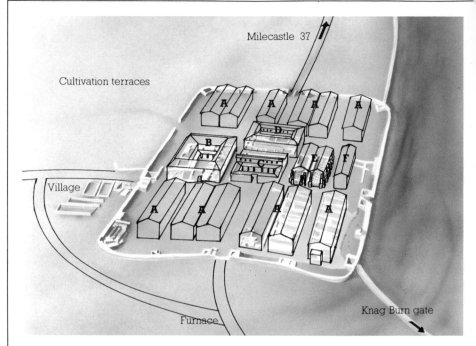

Cultivation terraces

Milecastle 37

Village

Furnace

Knag Burn gate

north–south, and the hard rock made it impossible to construct a strongroom or sink a well. A thousand infantrymen were stationed at Housesteads; it was a busy and strategically important posting and must have seen regular action. Excavations have uncovered unusual features such as a military hospital to the west of the headquarters building, but in recent years it has been the communal latrines that have attracted most attention, particularly from the hundreds of school groups who visit the place.

The reason Housesteads is justly famous has as much to do with its fine setting as its excavated walls. A short walk westward along Hadrian's Wall brings you to one of the most photographed views in England, looking east from Hotbank Crag

A two-and-a-half-mile drive west from Housesteads car park brings you to a staggered junction where a minor road crosses the Military Road. A right turn brings you to the line of the wall again, to Steel Rigg car park (NY 791677) from where there are excellent walking routes, either eastward past recently excavated sections of the wall, Castle Nick milecastle, and Crag Lough, or westward along the highest ridge of the Whin Sill at Winshields Crag. Turning left off the Military Road

Housesteads as a Roman architect might have visualized it.

A Barracks
B Commandant's house
C H.Q.
D Hospital
E Granary
F Workshop

at the junction brings you to the National Park Information Centre at Once Brewed (NY 753669). A few hundred yards further south along this side road there is a left turn leading to Vindolanda Roman Fort (NY 771664), an essential place to visit even though it was not a part of the wall defences. The original fort was built in the days of Agricola but its frontier role on the Stanegate meant that it was considerably modified, enlarged and rebuilt five times before being made redundant. Although the fort itself has not been fully excavated, the civilian settlement which grew up beside the fort has produced some of the most exciting and significant finds in Roman Britain, and many of these are on display in the nearby museum. Close to the museum building there is a Roman milestone, and close to the excavated ruins there is a replica of part of Hadrian's Wall, something missing from anywhere else in the wall area.

On the Military Road again and past the Once Brewed (a youth hostel) and the Twice Brewed (an inn), a two-and-a-half-mile drive brings you to another junction with the Milecastle Inn on the left and a turn to Cawfields on the right. Cawfields car park (NY 713667) offers a pleasant picnic site and a

Replicas of Hadrian's Wall at Vindolanda. These short sections, in both turf and stone, give a unique impression of the wall at its full height.

The River Irthing, here covered in ice and snow, marks the western boundary of the national park. To the west is the Cumbrian border and the remains of Birdoswald Roman Fort.

good starting point for walking either eastwards, past one of the best of the milecastles (on broad foundations with stones standing seven or eight courses high) and with excellent views of the vallum, or westward to Great Chesters fort. Great Chesters (NY 704668) was built to guard the Caw Gap and, like Housesteads, it lies on an east–west axis along the side of the wall. Few stones are visible; indeed, it is possible to walk past or even over the grassy mounds of the ramparts without realizing anything special is there, but it has several interesting features, particularly a six-mile aqueduct which brought water from the Haltwhistle Burn to within 350 yd (320 m) of the fort.

From the Cawfields turn the Military Road continues west to Greenhead. Just before the village there is a right turn which leads to the Museum of the Roman Army (NY 667658), close to the unexcavated site of the Stanegate fort known as Carvoran. Close by is both the boundary of the national park and the Cumbrian border. Beyond Greenhead the B6318 runs through Gilsland, over the River Irthing, and near to Birdoswald Roman Fort, an interesting but only partly excavated site which is also reputed to be where King Arthur died in battle

In Cumbria less of Hadrian's Wall has survived and the scenery is quite different, much less severe and less in keeping with the romantic image of the wild frontier of Rome.

In mid-Northumberland the busy A68 follows the line of Dere Street for many miles, detouring here and there to avoid difficult ridges, river-crossings or farm buildings. It is possible to drive right along the road without noticing anything Roman; there are no uncovered excavations north of Corbridge, no visitor services, no road signs. Virtually everything lies buried or half-hidden, often on private land or with poor access. Yet the ghost of the Roman road and its associated forts, camps, milestones and burial mounds are still visible across the landscape, and a twenty-five-mile drive from Corbridge to High Rochester provides an unusual alternative to better known wall country.

The Roman settlement at Corbridge, guarding the bridge over the Tyne and the crossroads of Dere Street and the Stanegate, was an important supply base and civilian community and makes a convenient starting point for an afternoon on Dere Street. The excavated remains of Corstopitum (NY 982649) are extensive and there is an excellent museum showing some of the finds. These include the famous Corbridge lion.

From Corstopitum drive into Corbridge village, then head north along the A68, steep and tree-lined until Stagshaw Bank is reached. Cross the roundabout and continue for a mile or two over the brow of the ridge. At this point there is an excellent view of the straight Roman road stretching ahead. Eleven miles to the north of Corbridge the road passes the Tone Inn; another mile further on is Waterfalls where a Roman milestone was reputedly used as a meeting place for rebel forces in the 1715 uprising. The landscape opens out with Chesterhope Common ahead. Just after a crossroads (Bellingham to the west, Sweethope to the east) the road descends towards Fourlaws Farm. At this point the A68 arcs to the right and Dere Street can be made out on the hillside as it continues straight ahead. Before the bend, on the left, is a large gateway to a private road, and close to this is a small gateway which gives access to the Roman camp of Swine Hill (NY 905825). The grass-covered square mound reveals little of its ramparts and gateways but the view, particularly of the North Tyne Valley to the west, is excellent.

After leaving Dere Street to detour through

Ridsdale, the A68 descends again towards West Woodburn. An old railway line cuts across the road half way down the hill, and close to the cutting there is a track leading south to Parkhead Farm. The ridge between the track and the main road has been quarried since Roman times and a figure known as Robin of Risingham (actually a Roman hunting god called Cocidius) once graced the rock face (NY 902856). Unfortunately the great block of 'slidden' sandstone on which the four-foot high figure was carved was cut up for gateposts by a spiteful farmer and all that now remains of Robin is his legs. A small reconstruction close by is poor compensation for the loss of the original.

Through West Woodburn and up the steep hillside, the A68 rejoins Dere Street and a scenic lay-by provides an opportunity to look back over the valley of the Rede. This is the best place to view the Roman fort of Habitancum, visible as a square green plateau a few hundred yards to the west of the road on the opposite bank of the Rede. Habitancum was an important outpost fort, garrisoned in the early third century by well trained cavalry and scouts called the *Exploratores Habitancensis*. Not far from the lay-by, close to a gateway and tumulus

An aerial view of the River Rede, and Habitancum Roman Fort.

Robin of Risingham. This reconstruction stands close to the remains of the original carving. The figure is Cocidius, the Roman hunting god.

to the west of the road, is a Roman milestone. Continuing along the border of the national park with the moorland of Corsenside and Troughend Common on the left, the straight and undulating road crosses Dargues Burn and passes a fenced platform of improved grassland, the extensive but barely discernible remains of Dargues Roman Camp. A little further on, as the road bears right, there are the more obvious grassy ramparts of Blakehope Fort (NY 857946), a very early four-acre, single-ditch fort which was probably built to guard the bridge over the Rede above Elishaw. The present bridge lies to the east of the Roman crossing place.

North of Elishaw Bridge, the A68 is joined by the A696 from Newcastle; Dere Street continues north west and from here to the Border there are eight temporary camps used by Roman road-builders and stop-over troops. At Rochester a small concealed side-road on the right leads uphill to High Rochester and the outpost fort of Bremenium (NY 833987). Its strategic position, at a road junction and overlooking the Sills Burn, probably makes this the most important of the Roman remains in Northumberland north of the wall, but its present appearance would hardly support this conclusion. The side-road actually cuts through the ramparts of the fort and peters out in a wide grassy platform with a scatter of houses and farm machinery. Thus the five-acre enclosure of the fort is no more than a village green. Stones from the fort have been used extensively to build bastles (fortified farmhouses), barns and field walls, and in more recent times to decorate the porch of the old school back at the road junction – another example of calculated vandalism by landowners. Bremenium ('Place of the Roaring Stream') was first built by Agricola on his northern campaign, long before the wall was thought of. The visible remains date back to the third century when the fort housed a thousand cavalry and the *Exploratores Bremeniensis*.

Half a mile south of the fort and overlooking Dere Street there is a circular stone tomb, probably commemorating an officer attached to the garrison of Bremenium. Nearby are three depressions in the ground which mark the sites of tombs excavated in the mid-nineteenth century, the stones long removed for wall-building. On the surviving tomb there are carvings of a pine cone and a deer head, symbols of death nearly worn away by time.

From Rochester, the A68 finally deserts Dere

Street and makes for the Border at Carter Bar. The Roman road does not take the easy ground and heads instead across the lonely hills to Coquetdale to the north. Either turn back to Corbridge at this point or detour round the block of hills. This is a lengthy procedure but if time permits it is possible to pick up Dere Street at its most dramatic by driving through Otterburn, Elsdon and Alwinton

Lines in the wilderness reveal the extent of Roman marching camps at Chew Green.

and making for the head of Coquetdale beyond Fulhope. In this wilderness stands Chew Green (NT 78–08–), a group of Roman camps and earthworks, with Gamel's Path (an ancient trackway) to the south and a Roman signal station on the Border Ridge to the north. To many people this place evokes the clearest impression of Roman achievement and futility; over 300 years of occupation are recorded in the landscape as a few mounds of grass-covered rubble.

What of the native population, the Celtic farmers who had watched with apprehension as the Romans settled down to a permanent occupation? The presence of anything up to 30,000 foreign troops must have had a dramatic effect on the rural economy, though it took years for the *Pax Romana* to achieve social integration even close to the forts. The Votadini people do not seem to have posed a threat to the invading army and were probably left to their own devices to come to terms with the new order. The impressive hillforts of the late Iron Age gave way to undefended settlements. These were still situated on moderately high ground, often on south-east slopes protected from prevailing winds. The main concentrations of these 'Romano-British'

Aerial photograph of a Romano-British farming settlement at Smalesmouth in North Tynedale.

settlements in the national park are on the hill crests above major valleys in the Cheviots, and along the North Tyne and the Rede. Usually, each settlement comprised a walled enclosure (oval in the Cheviot examples, rectangular in those further south) containing a huddle of five or six round stone-built houses fronted by a scooped or levelled stock yard. The grass-covered foundations of these structures are still easy to make out at such sites as Haystack Hill (NU 005150) and Redeswood Law (NY 863826). Often, Romano-British settlements were established within the defences of previous hillforts. At Greaves Ash above the Breamish Valley (NT 965164) and Lordenshaws above Rothbury (NZ 054993), circles of stone rubble reveal where dwellings spilled out over the demolished walls and on to the adjacent platform of land, suggesting a peaceful, thriving community.

It is possible that there was an increase in population at this time; there was certainly an extensive clearance of woodland to make way for crops and pasture. Analysis of pollen preserved in the peat bogs of sites throughout the national park (for example, Broad Moss above the Harthope Valley in the Cheviots) shows that this clearance was widespread and probably began in the early years of the occupation. Barley, rye and wheat were the cereals grown; perhaps a large proportion of this formed the 'tribute' exacted by the Romans and was used to feed the troops. Each soldier was allowed about two pounds of wheat per day, or a similar ration of barley if he was being punished!

Until quite recently it was thought that the northern uplands were inhabited by wandering herdsmen ('Celtic cowboys'), but it now seems likely that the Romano-British farmers developed a pastoral strategy remarkably similar to the inbye/outbye system employed in the Northumberland hills today. Enclosed fields close to farms or settlements were used to grow hay or crops, whilst cattle and sheep were moved from stock yards to hill pasture as the grazing conditions and seasons changed. The ghosts of these long-lost field systems disappear with the shallowest ploughing, but several have been discovered in recent years by aerial surveys of undisturbed Cheviot grasslands and can be traced on winter and spring landscapes. Examples are to be found at Brands Hill, Ilderton (NT 980247) and Knock Hill near Ingram (NT 998171). The fields are comparatively large (up to fifty acres) and there are remnants of walled drove roads leading from the stock yards through the fields to the rough pasture.

The Roman army gained many of its recruits from the local community; farmers' sons made ideal soldiers and the pay was good. Thus in the latter days of the occupation a significant proportion of the wall garrison would have been made up of men who knew no other homeland. Add to this the host of craftsmen, tradesmen, wives and prostitutes who lived in *vici* or villages around the forts and it is obvious that at the last there was little to separate the occupying army and the Celtic inhabitants of the area. The local economy must have been underpinned by the military presence, but there is no evidence for dramatic or violent change. Perhaps the farmers' sons simply returned home to take up the plough in what was now a more cultured and cultivated land.

5 **Saxon kings and Norman lords**

The lull following the breakdown of Roman administration lasted longer in the north of England than it did in the south; raiding parties from Frisia, Denmark and the lower Rhine had threatened the East Coast in the latter days of the occupation and this tide had increased to an irresistible flood by the turn of the sixth century. Settlement by these 'warrior farmers' had concentrated on the fertile lowlands, but in 547 an Angle chieftain, Ida, won control of the coastal fortress called Din Guoaroy and established this as the capital for a new northern kingdom called Bernicia. The name of the fortress was changed to Bamburgh; according to the *Anglo-Saxon Chronicle* a 'hedge' (presumably some kind of palisade) was constructed around the site, the first reference in history to this most English of features. Bamburgh, then as now, dominated the

Bamburgh Castle. The strategic value of the site was recognized by the Romans, and in Anglo-Saxon times King Ida built a fortress here.

whole coast, but expansion inland was limited by
the hostility of the British tribes. It took another forty
years before their 'English' kingdom was secure
and the more numerous local British population
subdued.

Bernicia and its neighbouring kingdom Deira
were eventually united in the reign of King
Aethelfrith. He was succeeded by Edwin, one of
several charismatic leaders able to extend the
power and influence of the new kingdom of
Northumbria. Edwin married a Christian princess of
Kent, Ethburge. A combination of her subtle
prompting and a dissatisfaction with the heathen
gods persuaded him to put the case for Christianity
to his council. According to Bede's *History of the
English Church and People*, one of his chief men
spoke eloquently in favour of enlightenment,
comparing the life of man with 'the swift flight of a
single sparrow through the banqueting-hall where
you are sitting at dinner on a winter's day with your
thanes and councillors. In the midst there is a
comforting fire to warm the hall; outside, the storms
of winter rain or snow are raging. This sparrow flies
swiftly in through one door of the hall, and out
through the other. While he is inside, he is safe from
the winter storm; but after a few moments of
comfort, he vanishes from sight into the wintry
world from which he came. . . .'

The council was convinced and Edwin was
baptized in 627, the eleventh year of his reign. This
heralded not only a religious and cultural revival,
but also a period of peace and stability. So much so
that 'a woman could carry her new-born babe
across the island from sea to sea without any fear or
harm'.

Edwin spent most of his time at York, but he
maintained other palaces in his kingdom, at
Edinburgh ('Edwin's Burgh'), and at Ad Gefrin on
the valley land of the River Glen (NT 926305), on
what is now the northern boundary of the national
park. The palace had been a fortress, expanded and
adapted by Aethelfrith into a residence fit for a king
and his court. Edwin had a church built to replace
what had probably been a pagan temple close to the
main palace structure, and Paulinus, his wife's
mentor and a celebrated missionary, who had
baptized Edwin in York, came up to spend thirty-six
days at Ad Gefrin baptizing his subjects. According
to Bede the 'people . . . gathered from all the
surrounding villages and countryside; and when he
[Paulinus] had instructed them, he washed them in

the cleansing waters of Baptism in the nearby River Glen'.

The exact site of Ad Gefrin was only discovered and excavated in the 1950s, for all the buildings were of wood and any earthworks had been completely levelled. A rather ugly roadside memorial on the B651 marks the spot. The Iron Age fort of Yeavering Bell (the word 'Yeavering' is derived from 'Ad Gefrin') overlooks the palace site; the two stand in full view of each other, part of the same landscape yet worlds apart in the roots of their cultures. The selection of the valley site is indicative of the Anglo-Saxons' 'village mentality'. The British kept to the wild hills, the English farmers to the cultivated valleys. Celtic names survived in topographical features such as hills ('Cheviot') and rivers ('Tyne') but settlements were given English names ('Elsdon', 'Kidland'); and the English language came into common usage.

Yeavering Bell, as seen from the Glen Valley close to the site of Ad Gefrin.

When Edwin died he left a virile Northumbria in ascendence over the southern kingdoms. As so often happens in history, however, the strength of the northern kingdom had been a reflection of its leader; there was a severe reversal as his immediate successors lost vital battles, and their lives, fighting the British king Cadwallon and the Mercian prince Penda. Northumbria fell apart.

Fortunately there was another hero waiting in exile, and at the battle of Heavenfield, close to Hexham, Christianity was set back on course by Oswald, son of Aethelfrith. The heathens were routed and Cadwallon killed. One of Oswald's first acts after his victory of 634 was to ask the Scottish elders for a bishop from Iona. They sent him Aidan, a good choice, energetic and honest, and quick to establish an episcopal see on the island of Lindisfarne. Unfortunately he could not speak English and Oswald had to translate his Scottish sermons so that the Northumbrian thanes could understand the teachings. Before long the floodgates were open, however, and every corner of Oswald's kingdom had been visited by a preacher of the Celtic church. Wooden churches began to appear. Henceforth Christianity was not to be denied. Oswald's death after less than a decade made little difference to the tide of civilization and learning. Aidan was followed by Finan and eventually by Cuthbert, a cult figure to the people of the North East. The influence of Northumbria grew; the Lindisfarne Gospels survive as an outstanding example of the heights reached in culture during the sixth and seventh centuries.

Yeavering palace as it would have been in Anglo-Saxon times.

The earthly lives of men and women in hill-farming communities were hardly influenced by events in cloisters and libraries, but religion was becoming important to them. Where there was no church or resident priest, crosses were erected to gather people to regular worship. Stone bases for these elegant crosses can be seen today at such places as Whittingham and Thockrington, and an impressive fragment of a cross shaft, ornately carved, can be seen in All Saints Church, Rothbury.

Throughout the Anglo-Saxon period the hills and moors of Northumberland were thinly populated and were renowned only for their sheep. People built in wood and were illiterate, so no record exists of their achievements. The only earthwork to inspire a second glance is the Black Dyke. This shallow ditch and bank runs from Bardon Mill to the confluence of the North Tyne and High Carriteth Burn. Perhaps it was built to mark a temporary limit of the English kingdom, linking features that had been selected as boundary marks. The best places to see the dyke are above Muckle Moss, just south of the park boundary, and from the Whin Sill at Sewingshields (NY 799700). But be warned; it is not an impressive or obvious feature and does not bear

The ruins of Lindisfarne Priory. In the distance, across the little harbour called 'The Ouse', is Lindisfarne Castle.

comparison with Offa's boundary between Mercia and the Welsh kingdoms.

Inevitably the power of Northumbria began to ebb; constant rivalry with the Mercians and Scots was nothing compared with the trauma of Viking raids on the windswept Northumberland coast. Lindisfarne, the jewel of Northumbrian achievement, was attacked and pillaged by the Danes in 793. In 873, following further coastal raids, the monks finally left Lindisfarne, taking with them their most sacred relics. But this only highlighted their plight; nowhere was safe. They spent years carrying the miraculously preserved corpse of St Cuthbert from place to place, terrified of the Danes to the east and the Norse to the west. Eventually the saintly burden was laid to rest at Durham, but many crags and shelters in the hills bear the diminutive of his name and are supposed to have been used as temporary refuges. Cuddy's Crag on the Whin Sill near Housesteads (NY 786688) is a typical example.

Chivalry and integrity were not entirely extinguished in these years; witness the conveyance of an area of land at Roddam on the national park boundary to the north of Ingram. The land was bequeathed by King Athelstan to Paulan Roddam.

> 'I, Kyng Adelstan
> giffs here to Paulan
> Oddan and Roddan
> als gud and als fair
> as evyr thai myne war
> and that to wytness
> Mald my wiffe'

By the end of the tenth century Lothian had been ceded to the emerging kingdom of Scotland and a blueprint for the present Border established. Once-proud Northumbria had become an earldom of the Danelaw, accepting new settlers with an uneasy grace. Pollen records for sites in the national park indicate considerable forest clearance at about this time, suggesting that the native population was obliged to open up marginal land.

The density of population in the Northumberland hills in pre-Conquest times was still very small however; a fraction of that in the more fertile and peaceful South. But a farming pattern in the hills and valleys was firmly fixed and was to evolve in a beleaguered state through centuries of Border warfare.

Cuddy's Crag, along the Whin Sill to the west of Housesteads Fort, is one of the most famous and photographed sections of Hadrian's Wall. The word 'cuddy', which appears on maps all over Northumberland, refers to Saint Cuthbert.

The Border troubles began as a royal dispute between proud nations and degenerated over the years into a squalid tangle of family feuds, theft and murder.

The foundations of a feudal society had already been established on the Border by the time William the Conqueror gained the throne, but there were still far-reaching changes in store. From the start, William mistrusted the North – and with justification. In 1069 he was obliged to move quickly to York to put down a rebellion inspired by Danes and Northumbrians, after which as a reprisal he set a torch to every field and dwelling between York and Durham and prevented any crops being grown for nearly a decade. According to Symeon of Durham 'so great a famine prevailed that men, compelled by hunger, devoured human flesh, that of horses, dogs and cats, and whatever custom abhors'.

Refugees fled north across the Scottish border and Northumberland became a virtual desert. William destroyed evey town except Bamburgh, then spent two weeks on the Border checking its security before heading south via Harbottle and Hexham – an unusual route that took him through Upper Coquetdale. He was back on the Border in less than a year however, this time intent on settling the question of whose kingdom was to become the dominant power. Malcolm of Scotland was no match for him and he lost the encounter. The Normans must have thought the defeat and 'submission' of Malcolm was the end of the matter, but it merely aggravated the Scottish sense of injustice and was a prelude to much worse problems from the thirteenth to sixteenth centuries.

William took over and augmented the existing social and fiscal organization in Northern England, added new taxes, and ensured that everyone rendered service and added to his wealth. He appointed a Norman earl of Northumberland to protect his interest in the area, but on the troublesome Borderlands he trusted to the self-interest of his barons, granting them 'liberties' – small 'regalities' within which the king's writ did not run. The Tynedale liberty was not created until the twelfth century, but the important liberty of Redesdale, which included much of Upper Coquetdale and therefore a large part of what is now the national park, was given by William to his friend Robert de Umfraville. The only condition to the gift was that he defended Redesdale 'from enemies and wolves with that sword which King William had by his side when he entered Northumberland'.

All William wanted of Northumberland and its inhospitable hills was that it should be kept quiet and act as a buffer. He did not visit the area again and his Domesday Survey of 1086 did not include the barren Borderlands. In subsequent years his descendants had to suffer occasional incursions by Scottish kings but the cultural and diplomatic ties between the two countries were close and gradually the desert of the north showed signs of recovery and even prosperity.

Robert de Umfraville's descendants proved to be strong and competent Marcher lords. In their early years they established themselves at Elsdon, the key settlement and nerve-centre for Redesdale, and built a motte and bailey castle on the ridge above Elsdon Burn (NY 939935). The surviving earthwork, considered one of the finest of its period, is easy to view from the main road or, more impressively, from the adjacent hills. After a few years the de Umfravilles decided that the position of Elsdon was a little too vulnerable and transferred their seat to Harbottle in Upper Coquetdale. This latter site became the base for subsequent lords of the March

An aerial view of Elsdon. The village is grouped around an extensive green and enclosed churchyard (see picture page 69). Behind the church is a pele tower (see picture page 73), whilst at the far side of the village is a Norman motte and bailey.

when the de Umfravilles moved again to a still finer castle at Prudhoe. The original structure of Harbottle Castle was made of wood but was rebuilt in stone; the earthwork foundations can be seen to the north of the road through Harbottle village, on a spur created by the River Coquet (NT 932048). That so little remains is a silent testament to the persistence of the Scots.

Other important families with land on the Border included the de Vescys of Alnwick who owned an extensive estate embracing Alnham, Prendwick and Biddlestone, and the Muschamps of Wooler. The latter held a barony centred on Wooler and were lords of 'the free forest of Chyviot'. An earthwork known locally as 'the cup and saucer' marks the site of an early motte, but this was deserted in favour of a stone castle close to the much later structure of St Mary's church in Wooler.

Stone churches began to appear in several villages in the Norman period though none has remained intact or without subsequent modification. Ingram, Alnham, Ilderton and Kirknewton churches have varying degrees of original stonework and all are full of character. The political influence of the Church increased considerably under Norman patronage; favoured bishops were at least as important as barons. In the hill country of Northumberland one sign of the diversification of the Church's interests was of incalculable importance and not merely for religious or social reasons. In 1157 a Cistercian abbey was founded at Newminster on the Wansbeck near Morpeth; this was an offshoot of the more famous abbey of Fountains. Cistercians were pastoral entrepreneurs,

and as at Fountains their prosperity was based on wool. Grazing rights were established across Kidland and the Cheviots and a fulling mill was built at Barrow Burn (NT 867107). Sheep breeding, for long the pride of the better drained uplands, became all-pervasive and was largely responsible for the evolution of the treeless 'wastes' noted by travellers in succeeding centuries.

Around the villages arable land was cultivated on an open-field system involving the sub-division of two or three large fields into a series of narrow strips. These strips, known locally as 'riggs', were always ploughed in a clockwise direction so that the earth was banked slightly to the right, creating a ridge on one side and a trough on the other. The 'rigg and furrow' within a field was usually aligned so that water drained down the troughs and off the cultivated areas: effective and simple. It required the village community to work together since each rigg was tenanted by a different person and no individual could afford his own ox team. Gradually more and more land was taken into cultivation and there are places in the national park today where whole hillsides, now swathed in grass, heather or spruce trees, exhibit the tell-tale corrugated surface created by this medieval cultivation.

Kirknewton church, on the northern boundary of the national park, close to the confluence of the College Burn, River Glen and Bowmont Water.

Deserted villages and field systems at such places as Hartside (NT 985176) and Leafield Edge (NT 985135) are numerous and suggest that the population in the Cheviot hills was higher in the thirteenth century than it had ever been before and was ever to be again. Beyond the busy villages and fields there remained the waste. Cattle or sheep belonging to the villagers could not be sustained in the immediate area for long, particularly with the increasing need for arable land. Thus a system developed whereby the herds and flocks were driven each spring into the hills to graze on wild grass and heather. Herdsmen went too, staying all summer in small huts or 'shielings' in the traditional 'shieling grounds' and returning to the security of the farm or village in the autumn. The stock was then let loose on the stubble or fed on hay for the winter. This system survived in the remoter Northumberland hills for much longer than it did elsewhere in England, and was still noted in Elizabethan times by William Camden who visited Redesdale in 1599:

> 'Here every way round in the wasts as they tearme them, you may see as it were the ancient Nomades, a martiall kinde of men, who from the moneth of Aprill into August, lye out scattering and summering (as they tearme it) with their cattell in little cottages here and there which they call Sheales and shealings.'

The names of many isolated hill dwellings still bear the stamp of this system of transhumance ('Longheugh*shields*', NY 821847; 'Wolfer*shiel*' NU 012004). The word 'hope', liberally scattered over maps of the high hills, denotes an area of sheltered grazing, hence 'Langleeford Hope' in the Harthope Valley (NT 933208) was the summer grazing associated with Langleeford (NT 964233) lower down the valley. Only a small proportion of the old thatched huts grew into permanent dwellings however, and hills are littered with their ruins. Ultimately the shieling tradition proved to be self-destructive, for the longer it lasted the more impoverished people became. Fathers divided their holdings equally among their sons, so each generation had less to live on. The population was increasing. There was no incentive to improve the quality of the summer grazing since it was shared and the climate was deteriorating to what is now called the Little Ice Age. And there was always the

The wild white cattle of Chillingham Park.

likelihood of being robbed of stock by 'reivers' or 'moss-troopers' from either side of the Border. The seeds of both poverty and lawlessness were being sown.

Whilst farmers and husbandmen wrested a living from the unpromising soil, Norman barons and Marcher lords indulged their passion for hunting. Four great forests existed, Lowes (north of Hadrian's Wall), Redesdale, Rothbury and Cheviot. A 'forest' in those days was not necessarily covered with trees but 'beasts of the chase' needed cover and the necessary habitat, usually a mosaic of wood, grass and wetland, was conserved. Strict forest laws ensured that villagers were not tempted to poach the King's deer, but they were usually allowed to cut brushwood and to graze their pigs on the pannage of the forest floor. In 1199 King John granted all the rights to Redesdale forest to Richard de Umfraville, and in 1205 he granted similar rights, of the chase, pasture, vert and venison in Rothbury forest, to Robert Fitz-Roger. In later years a new fashion for park deer (ie, fallow rather than red) saw the enclosure of suitably wooded areas into walled parks; the drystone wall to the north of Lordenshaws marks the boundary of Fitz-Roger's deer park established towards the end of the thirteenth century. This was also the time the wild white cattle of nearby Chillingham were enclosed in parkland, ensuring the survival of what were probably semi-wild descendants of aurochs.

6 **Border troubles**

Lasting peace on the border was a dream rather than a reality. The individual strength of England and Scotland ensured mutual respect but prudent landowners on either side began to build tower-houses of impenetrable stone. Their pessimism was well founded. One dark evening in March 1286, King Alexander III of Scotland fell off his horse and broke his neck and the country was suddenly faced with an uncertain future. The throne passed to his grand-daughter but she died only a few years later and there was a dispute about the succession. This was exactly what Edward I of England had been waiting for and in 1296 he was able to engineer the accession of a puppet king, John Balliol, to the Scottish throne. Unfortunately Balliol proved less than honourable to his patron and tried to negotiate an alliance with France. Edward marched north, crushed Balliol with apparent ease, and left Scotland to lick her wounds under the watchful control of a governing army. But this was not a lasting victory and the occupying army was itself destroyed by a Scottish force under William Wallace, who then dispatched a raiding party to lay waste to Northumberland, not for the first or last time. People quickly learned that their former friends and neighbours had a darker side and before very long there was a deep emnity between the Borderers. The victory of Robert Bruce over Edward II at Bannockburn in 1314 ensured the independence of the Scottish nation but did nothing for any long-term prospects for peace. Neither side showed mercy or consideration for those living in the Marches and frequent raiding parties left utter destruction and terror in their wake. If this was not bad enough there was also widespread crop failure and an outbreak of the Black Death which arrived in the North East via Sunderland in 1349. Not surprisingly the confidence of the local population was shattered and the land 'brought forth nothing but misery'. Cultivation in the higher valleys came to an abrupt halt, herdsmen were less inclined to risk their lives in the wastes, and the bustling drove roads like Clennel Street, which crossed the remote Cheviot ridge from Scotland, fell silent.

The troubled state of the Border continued for 300 years and had a devastating effect on agrarian progress. Several battles were fought between English and Scottish forces in the fourteenth and fifteenth centuries. Armies led by earls and lords were encouraged by their respective kings to instigate raids and weaken the opposing Borderlands. The most famous of these battles was at Otterburn in 1388 when a Scottish force under the Earl Douglas met an English force led by Harry Hotspur, son of Henry Percy, the Earl of Northumberland. The fight took place at night with Hotspur's men tired after a forced march, and the result was a resounding victory for the Scots. The encounter is vividly described in one of the finest ballads in the English language, 'The Battle of Otterburn', which begins by setting the rural scene and the Scottish intention:

> 'Yt fell obowght the lamasse tyde,
> Whan husbonds wynn their haye,
> The dowghtye Douglasse bowynd him to ryde,
> In Yngland to take a praye.'

Douglas had a premonition of the outcome of the battle:

> 'But I hae dreamed a dreary dream,
> Beyond the Isle of Sky,
> I saw a dead man win a fight,
> And I think that man was I.'

Sure enough, Douglas died in victory whilst Hotspur was captured in defeat and later ransomed. Over 1,000 Englishmen were taken prisoner or killed; the dead were buried at Elsdon church. Close to where Earl Douglas met his death is 'Percy's Cross', a tall stone pillar which rests on the socket of the original 'Battle Stone' (NY 877936). Unfortunately the place is now shrouded in a small forest plantation and has lost much of its atmosphere.

Hotspur gained his revenge over the Douglas clan in the autumn of 1402 at the battle of Humbleton Hill (NT 96–28–). The battle is commemorated by the Bendor Stone in a field by the B6351, but the main fight took place between Humbleton Hill and Harehope Hill and it is possible to walk these fine slopes and gain a much better impression of the lie of the land. According to the *Annales Henrici* 'They [the Scots] took a hill near to the place where our

The casualties from the battle of Otterburn lie beneath the turf of St Cuthbert's churchyard at Elsdon.

men were stationed. Our men, seeing this, took another hill [Harehope], and so a valley lay between the two hosts. Meanwhile a band of 500 archers, who had gone forth that night to forage, returned; and when they saw the two battles drawn upon the hills, they suddenly determined to attack and sent a number of their archers to shoot against the Scottish lines and entice them to descend'. Archibald Douglas attacked the English and forced them to give way, but Hotspur's Welsh archers delivered 'so heavy a volley that their arrows pierced the armour and broke the swords and lances of the enemy. The Douglas himself was wounded five times despite the magnificence of his armour. The rest of the Scots who had not yet descended from the hill fled; some were slain by archers, some captured and others put to death'. Of Douglas's force of 10,000, over 800 were killed on the battlefield and another 500 drowned in the River Tweed. But Hotspur did not survive long to savour his triumph; he quarrelled with his king, Henry IV, about the ransom due to him for Douglas and his Scottish knights, and this led to Hotspur's revolt and the battle of Shrewsbury in which he was killed.

Perhaps justice was done, but the feud between the Percy and Douglas families continued, as did a host of lesser clan disputes.

This kind of institutionalized violence was only a whisper away from lawlessness and the continual 'reiving' by bands of farmer thieves undermined security so much that the Border was split into different Marches, each under a lord appointed by the king to mete out justice and retribution. Both the Scottish and English sides of the Border had a West, Middle and East March, and the lords of the Marches would meet to discuss any pressing problems with their opposite numbers and a small group of supporters or arbiters. But even these meetings were not free of treachery and had to be carefully organized in remote passes or 'gates'. Russell's Cairn, a Bronze Age monument on the wild border ridge at Windy Gyle (NT 855152) marks one of these places and is named after Lord Francis Russell who was killed at a Wardens' Meeting in 1585. A few years earlier Russell had been present at a meeting at Redeswire (Carter Bar) and had been taken captive after a bloody confrontation between Sir John Forster of the Middle March and Sir John Carmichael, Keeper of Liddesdale, at which the Deputy Warden had been murdered. These were supposed to be the most honourable and just men in the Borders.

The Middle March had by far the worst reputation; it comprised most of what is now the national park, stretched from Kershopefoot to the Hanging Stone on Cheviot, and included the infamous areas of North Tynedale and Redesdale. According to surveys of the mid-sixteenth century, Tynedale was 'plenished ... with wild and misdemeaned people' whilst the inhabitants of Redesdale 'do lykewyse delyte and use themselves in Theftes and spoyles'. In order to counter the unique problems of the Border a series of special Border laws evolved. These included the curious law of 'Hot Trodd' by which the victim of a raid was allowed, within a six-day period, to chase after the thieves and 'follow their lawful trod with hue and cry, with horn and hound' – and with smouldering peat or straw fixed to the end of their lance.

Sadly, the spurious justice, petitions and surveys only succeeded in giving the area a national reputation. In Elizabethan times, the celebrated traveller William Camden was too scared to go near the central section of Hadrian's Wall because of 'mosstroopers' who dwelt there. James I, on being

Russell's Cairn, on the
Border Ridge at Windy
Gyle.

told a banal story of a cow sent to market from
Scotland to London which managed to walk home
again afterwards, is reputed to have quipped that
'the most surprising part of the story you lay least
stress on, that she past unstolen through the
debatable land'.

Black humour could not hide the essential tragedy
of the Borders or the inability of either side to do
very much to improve matters, at least before the
Union of the Crowns in 1603. The spirit of the times
can be gleaned from this letter written by the
enthusiastic Warden of Middle March, Sir Robert
Carey, and sent to the lord treasurer, Lord
Burghley:

> 'On the 2^d instant a company of 200 Scots, 80 of
> them and more, armed with "calyvers and
> horsemens peeces" – came into England, their
> purpose unknown to me. I made all the force I
> could, and sent with speed to encounter them.
> And about 3 P.M. Mr Woodrington and Mr
> Fenwick whom I sent as leaders, set upon the
> Scots within England, and overthrew them.
> They were then so near their own borders, that
> they had "recovered Scotland" before we got
> to them. But the foray being broken, they held
> on the chase two miles into Scotland, and
> private men slew their enemies who were in
> deadly feud with them, as they came to them: so
> I think there are some 4 or 5 Scots slain, and 16
> of the best taken prisoners. After our men made
> a retreat, the prisoners were asked what their
> meaning was to enter the Queen's dominions
> with such force in warlike manner? They said

their only intent was to hunt, and take such venison as the country afforded. . . . They knew quite well it was unlawful. . . . But these men, though the chiefest of them have been great offenders to this March both in blood and goods, and that lately, chose to make this bravado. Besides their hunting, their custom is to bring in 100 men at these times, to cut and carry away wood and they have thus clean wasted ''one of the goodlyest woodes'' in the Middle March.'

In this confused atmosphere of corruption and duplicity, bravery and romance, there evolved the Border Ballads, a collection of evocative stories handed down over the centuries, popularized and bowdlerized by Sir Walter Scott, and enshrined in the Child Ballads. However, the practical legacy of these years of uncertainty was the poverty of both the people and the landscape. Most houses were built of wood and, since they were regularly burnt to the ground, trees became a valuable resource, as revealed in Sir Robert Carey's letter. Much of the Cheviot forest disappeared by gradual and clandestine clearance for building purposes, for which the Scots were always blamed. Even so, it was obvious to the more wealthy landowners that thick stone walls offered a much surer protection from 'reiving, riding Scots', and a rich heritage of defensive or semi-defensive buildings has survived.

No true castles were built in the Northumberland hills after Norman times; towards the coast the great castles of Bamburgh, Dunstanburgh and Warkworth were at their prime in Plantagenet and Tudor times but warring armies simply bypassed the inland hills and there was no need for a fortress in the middle of a wilderness. However, the local aristocracy, living in their comfortable manor houses in the shadow of the hills, felt the chill of the Scottish Wars of Independence, particularly the savage aftermath of Stirling and Bannockburn. They were quick to fortify their dwellings or even rebuild them.

Only ruined walls now remain of the large fourteenth-century tower-house at Thirlwall (NY 660662) and even less survives of the thirteenth-century structure at Tarset (NY 788855), but they demonstrate the early determination of wealthy landowners to defend their property against Border raids. Just outside the national park, excellent examples of fourteenth-century tower-houses form

A medieval sword dating from 1200 to 1350, found near Silloans in Upper Redesdale in 1986. The blade is of tempered steel and the iron pommel is gilded with copper. It is interesting to speculate on the circumstances of its loss – the owner would not have parted with it lightly.

the basis of imposing homes at Langley and Featherstone. Smaller tower-houses, often called pele-towers, were built in subsequent years by the lesser gentry who could not yet afford a high degree of protection. These peles were often surrounded by palisades or walls, protecting stock yards ('barmkins') into which the cattle and horses could be gathered and the dependents of the estate could take refuge. At the turn of the fifteenth century there were at least seventy-eight of these buildings in Northumberland. Priests required their own special fortified homes close to their churches and several 'parson's peles' have survived in good order, including those at Alnham (NT 990110) and Elsdon (NY 936934). Both have been renovated into private residences in recent years but give an excellent impression of the practical architecture of the Border wars: three or four storeys in height, eight-foot thick walls, and very small windows.

In more remote Border areas the mid-sixteenth century saw the appearance of a quite new defensive structure, a fortified farmhouse or 'bastle', and by 1650 several hundred of these dour rectangular buildings were scattered over the Borderlands. Virtually confined to the twenty-mile

The vicar's pele at Elsdon.

zone identified in an act of 1555 as in need of special
protection, they are a product of the very precise
requirements of more prosperous farmers for
security for their families and stock against small
raiding parties (the houses of poor tenants and
workers were still built of wood or turf). Bastles
were quite uniform in shape and structure and many
have survived almost unaltered. They usually
measure 35 ft by 25 ft (10.5 m by 7.5 m) have walls 4 ft
(1.2 m) thick, and contain two storeys beneath a
sharply pitched roof. The upper floor would have
accommodated the farmer and his family, the lower
would have housed cattle or other stock. Often
bastles were grouped together, or at least were
built within sight of one another, so that a farmer
could rely on the support of his neighbours if he
were attacked. The ghosts of the old bastles can be
found today in the shell of anything from a haybarn
to a public house, but the best intact examples are to
be seen at such places as Gatehouse (NY 788890)
and Black Middens (NY 775898). Ruins can be found
almost anywhere.

   After the union of the crowns, Northumberland
took many years to settle down to anonymity. Even
during the conflict there had been long periods of

Black Middens bastle in
North Tynedale.

peace but the years of war were never entirely
forgotten. Woodland was dwindling, the uplands
were a wilderness of heath and mire, and the
villages had contracted or been deserted. The key
to the present national park landscape lies in this
distant and troubled past.

Reconstruction of a
typical bastle-house.

7 The making of the modern landscape

Given a new king, a settled border and the will of both peasants and Percys, the mists gradually cleared from the Northumberland hills. It took some time for the amoral inhabitants of Tynedale and Redesdale to change their ways, to stop rustling sheep and cattle and try to make an honest living. Not only had they acquired a reputation for freebooting, they were also noted for their lack of sobriety and had developed a taste for whisky, unusual in England at this time. This habit seems to have taken even longer for the authorities to control and at the turn of the nineteenth century there were illicit 'stills' in several out-of-the-way places at the valley heads. Coquetdale was particularly well endowed. An inn with the unlikely name of Slyme Foot, at the confluence of the Rowhope Burn and the Coquet, did a roaring trade in what was called 'innocent whiskey'. Nothing remains of this venerated building except its reputation; a little further up Coquetdale, on the Inner Hare Cleugh close to the junction of Davidson's Burn (NT 887164) is the later ruin of Rory's Still, the kiln for drying malted barley still visible against the slope of the hill. 'Black Rory' was reputed to be a fiery Highlander. He was certainly industrious and he operated at least four other distilleries in the area to the west of Rothbury. Excisemen rarely troubled the hill country and the 'stills' were often substantial and far from hidden. Peat provided the fuel, barley was carted up from the lower valleys, and grey hens (casks) of whisky were carted back down to slake the thirst of the Border communities. Cross-border smuggling, to take advantage of the varying excise duty between England and Scotland, was considered a legitimate activity too, and very innocuous compared with what had gone before.

Droving, the herding south of many thousands of Scottish-reared cattle to London markets, was re-established right across the Borders and reached its zenith in the late eighteenth century. Well worn drove roads such as The Street, Clennel Street and Salter's Road, the latter so named because it had been established as a trade route for sea-salt from

The inconspicuous remains of Rory's Still lie in the shadows between the Border Ridge and Bloody Bush Edge.

the coast, can still be traced as 'green roads' across some of the finest hill country. They make excellent walking routes. The established drove roads were augmented by a host of secret gaps and causeways through heaths and mires, avoiding any tariffs and helping to earn for the drovers a buccaneering reputation for being 'shaggy, unkempt and wild as the cattle in their care'.

With Border defence no longer an imperative issue, landowners looked to the profitability of their estates. They no longer needed to gather men to the muster rolls or have a force ready to ride after reivers. This meant that the old feudal relationship lost much of its relevance and the profits to be made from wool, corn and coal seduced many landowners into turning out their customary tenants. Arable fields on the edges of the Cheviots were put down to new crops such as turnips (introduced in the middle of the eighteenth century) or were seeded with 'artificial grasses', and the commons were enclosed for rough grazing. Parliamentary enclosure awards, the seizing of traditional commons in the name of more efficient farming practices, were less fiercely opposed in the wastes of Northumberland than elsewhere because the rural population was at a very low ebb and there was an understandable reluctance to stand up to the lord of the manor.

Enclosure was taking place from the seventeenth century and gained pace through the eighteenth century; the award for over 10,000 acres of Elsdon Common is dated 1729. There were still large tracts of upland heath and moor being enclosed in the middle of the nineteenth century, for example, 6,000 acres of Rothbury forest in 1831. In the valleys and

lower hills the new fields were bounded by quick-set hedges. These were described in an innovative agricultural review in 1800 as 'earth mounds; at the base of which, and on the edge of the ditch out of which they are raised, are planted the quicks, generally upon a turned sod six inches high'. 'Quicks' – hawthorns – were used to the exclusion of virtually all other bushes because they were 'quick to set' and thoroughly stockproof if properly maintained. The same survey described how some farmers cut the hedges when still young and then trimmed them every year, whilst others left them to mature and laid them on a nine-or-ten-year rotation. According to the survey there was no comparison between the two methods 'in point of profit, and of labour saved . . . and for beauty, we prefer Nature and think a luxuriant hawthorn, in full bloom, or loaden with its ripeneing fruit, is a more pleasing, enlivening, and gratifying object than the stiff, formal sameness produced by the shears of a gardener'. These days many hedges are derelict having been allowed to grow out or to suffer the constant attention of sheep. Even those hedges that have been maintained suffer the 'formal sameness' induced by the mechanical flail.

Solitary hawthorn bushes and earthbanks are all that remain of many quickset hedges.

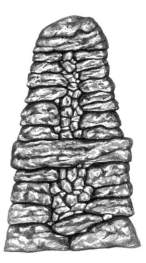

Drystone walling in the Cheviots near North Middleton.

Cross-section of a drystone wall, comprising coping stone, facing stones, infill, through stone and footings.

On the higher hills, the heather or grass-clad wastes, drystone walls or dykes were frequently built. At the time, people complained that they were unnatural and sliced the hills into geometric shapes, but they were a sensible solution to the problem of enclosing sheep walks and raw material was readily to hand either from small quarries or from the remains of prehistoric monuments. The skill of the drystone wallers in the nineteenth century, unrecognized in their lifetime, can be appreciated today in the apparent permanence of what they built, particularly the circular 'stells' or sheep-folds which are used extensively by hill shepherds to gather the hill flocks prior to shearing or dipping. However, time and the surprising climbing ability of sheep has meant that many walls are now no longer stock-proof, and although there are still a few drystone wallers at work it takes cash grants to encourage landowners to use them rather than employing a contractor to put in a post and wire fence.

The overdue reshaping of agriculture made possible by a peaceful Border gained momentum towards the end of the eighteenth century, due to increases in food prices and correspondingly high incentives to farmers to increase yields. It took a few far-sighted men such as George Culley of Glendale to show by example what could be achieved, but most farmers on the larger estates were ready to learn and seem to have been remarkably radical. 'Their minds are open to convictions – they are ready to try new experiments . . . many of them have traversed the most distant parts of the kingdom to obtain agricultural knowledge' (MacKenzie, 1811). This certainly applied to Culley. His greatest success in stock rearing was the introduction of the Leicester or 'Dishley' sheep. A farmer of these enlightening times was moved to write that 'previous to the improvements by the introduction of the ''Dishley'' breed the general breed of sheep were called *Mugs*, a name descriptive of their nature'.

By the middle of the nineteenth century, a separate breed had been evolved from the Dishley stock, called the Border Leicester, and this is still one of the most important breeds in the national park. The tup (ram) is crossed with a Cheviot ewe to produce half-breed lambs for fattening on lowland farms. Sheep have always been the mainstay of the hill-farming economy and the history of the breeds

A Blackface tup.

goes back several centuries. Two in particular were developed to suit the Border conditions; these were known as the 'Long Breed' and the 'Short Breed' (farmers were ever pragmatists rather than poets). The 'Long Breed' developed into the famous Cheviot, a neat, white-faced animal suited to the more sheltered and protected grasslands of the volcanic Northumberland hills. The 'Short' or 'heath' breed came to be known as the Blackface, a breed that seems to thrive on the 'black land', the heather-covered and windswept upper hills and moors. For many people the sight of flocks of Cheviots and 'blackies' is an integral part of a walk in the hills. But times change and the role of the Blackface, either as the unit of a sturdy hill flock or crossed with a blue-faced Leicester to produce 'mule' lambs, is gradually being taken over by the more hardy Swaledale. Some farmers and shepherds like to introduce some Swaledale blood into their Blackface flocks; the clue to this mixed parentage is the inheritance of the grey muzzle and rangy appearance of the Swaledale, detracting from the compact nature of the pure Blackface.

The shepherd whose job it was to care for the hill sheep used to live in small cottages high among the hills, often miles from the nearest road. Hill flocks are always 'hefted' to a particular 'cut', that is they develop a grazing pattern within an area they know well and are usually able to seek out adequate shelter from the worst of the winter. This habit is very useful to the shepherd but it means he is obliged to travel out to the flock over rough terrain, and until recently this meant he had to live close by.

Cattle overwintering on the open hills at Garleigh Moor.

Today most shepherds live in the main valleys and use motorbikes or tractors to get out on to the hills, not so romantic but much more sensible. They still use dogs of course; the first sheep dog trials ever held in Britain were at Byrness in 1866 and the Border area is still producing national champions.

Cattle were more widespread in the hills than they are now, but they were never the kind to gain a place in the affection of countrymen. Apart from one or two milkers for the benefit of the farmer and his family all the cattle were, and still are, reared for beef. Most originated from Ireland and were 'stores' let loose on the lower hillsides to fatten before selling them on again at Wooler or Rothbury marts. They were of indeterminate breed and were called 'Irish' cattle to cover a multitude of origins in their ancestry.

The move to improved cattle breeds came first with an increase in the number of black Galloways, then with the introduction of shorthorns in the late eighteenth century. The shorthorns were crossed with the Galloways to produce 'blue-grey' calves. These days, many of the smaller farms in the south and west of the national park still have herds of black or rust-coloured Galloways and their hairy grey offspring, and there are quite a lot of 'Irish' about too. In the north, and in particular in the Cheviots, there are fewer cattle but there has been greater investment by farmers who can afford to stock their wintering sheds with Aberdeen Angus heifers and serve them with Charolais or Limousin bulls.

As implied above, the eighteenth and nineteenth centuries brought a parting of the ways for farmers at opposite ends of the Northumberland hills. Estates and holdings in the south had been fragmented and split into small units, barely profitable. Today these same small farms, often owner-occupied, add greatly to the variety of the landscape but are still far from affluent. In the north most of the land was in the hands of prosperous estates and has remained so to this day. Individual farms usually cover a thousand or more acres and the tenants are able to use the latest technology and machinery, making their lives easier and their jobs more efficient.

At the turn of the nineteenth century there were 3,500 horses in Coquetdale alone. Of these, nearly 3,000 were draught animals. Clydesdales were popular, but on heavier soils the local 'Vardy' and 'Blackwell' breeds were considered to have greater

Some hill shepherds still use horses rather than motorbikes to get up on to the hills.

stamina. The modern eighty horsepower tractor does the same job in a fraction of the time without any need for a 'tush' or a slice of turnip. A few shepherds still use horses to take them out on their rounds, preferring their company and reliability to the noise and speed of a motorbike. Perhaps this says something for the style and aptitude of the hill shepherds, though by tradition the poorer classes were not credited with very much sense or intelligence. The rural workers were described by Mackenzie as 'employed principally in the innocent occupation of tending their bleating flocks upon the hills, and having little intercourse with the world, they retain strongly the vulgar opinions and local prejudices of their forefathers'. He described the peasants who worked the fields as a 'hardy race of men, capable of bearing considerable fatigue', but this patronizing attitude was probably based on his desire for the workforce to mirror the simple contented and thankful image portrayed of the working classes of his day. In fact the 'hinds' or farm labourers had a very hard life. They lived in a single room with access to a garden in which they could grow vegetables to supplement their diet. The farmer paid them 'in kind', usually based on a sack of grain to last a month, and the hind was obliged to supply an additional worker from his family to 'answer at all times his master's call, and to work at stipulated wages' (Grey, 1840). This system of 'bondage' survived well into the present century, though since the farm worker could not always supply the 'bondager' from his own family he often employed a fit and sturdy girl from the local village to do the job for a small wage and a handful of grain.

In lowland areas and foothills most farm workers were needed in the immediate vicinity of the farm rather than in hill cottages. Thus farms developed more like little villages or hamlets, a set of angular stone buildings clustered around a stock yard. Apart from the bastles of the seventeenth century, there are no really old farm buildings in the national park, mainly because everything prior to 1600 had been of a temporary nature, built of wattle and daub and easily replaced after Border raids. The rebuilding came gradually, as a result of the confidence of the eighteenth and nineteenth centuries, but even turf or heather-clad farmhouses of this period were rebuilt in Victorian times as the big estates worked towards model designs and greater efficiency. The new steadings reflected the size of the holdings and were modern in concept and design. This accounts today for the open landscape and low population in the hill country, and for the fact that buildings are still in use, often for their original purpose.

It was the overriding demand for building stone at this time that led to the destruction of many of the Roman remains and so angered antiquarians such as William Hutton who visited Hadrian's Wall in 1801. However, although Hutton was vitriolic about the vandalism inflicted by some farmers he was at least quick to appreciate any kindness at the hands of local people as he walked the wall: 'Although a public house, they had no ale, cyder, porter, beer, or liquors of any kind, except milk, which was excellent; but they treated me with something preferable, Civility.'

Small villages, which had sprung up in the lower valleys during Anglo-Saxon times, acted as the focus for the rural community, but where they had once served a defensive purpose they were now more important for their supportive trades and as a place for people to meet. In fact there are very few villages of any size within the national park; such places as Elsdon, Ingram and Kirknewton are really no more than hamlets gathered around a church or pele tower. The 'spiritual' lives of farm workers often revolved around their frequent visits to market where they could spend any cash in their pockets at the local inn. Here too Mackenzie had a suspiciously naïve view of country life: 'The market being over, the fiddlers take their seats close to the windows in the public-houses, the girls begin to file off and gently pace the streets, with a view to gaining admirers; while the young men, with equal innocent designs, follow after . . .'.

Many of the most engaging traditions associated with the Borders have survived as a result of the regular gathering together of the unusually isolated community. Stick-dressing, the art of creating a beautifully carved shepherd's crook from a sheep's horn and hazelwood, is the product of long lonely hours followed by a triumphant competition at one of the annual shepherds' shows. The Northumbrian pipes and the fiddle are still played at gatherings and club nights, though with the current 'folk-revival' many of the players are up from Newcastle for the evening to recover a small part of their heritage.

Very few of the hill farms in the national park grow arable crops. It is doubtful if many of those in

Stick-dressing – creating a finely worked crook or walking stick from a ram's horn and hazel rod.

the Hadrian's Wall area could, but in the north rye was grown in many of the valleys in the eighteenth century, as well as 'downy-chaffed' wheat. In Glendale, the district arcing around the north east of the Cheviots, good quality oats were grown extensively at the turn of the nineteenth century and were sold in London markets for up to 1/6d per quarter pound. But improvement again brought changes. The introduction of lime to the land meant that turnips replaced the rye and these days barley is the most extensive corn crop. In the go-ahead 1800s, threshing machines were driven either by horse-power, necessitating the construction of a wheel-house ('gin-gan '), or by steam.

Lime made a big difference to the 'sour' soils of the uplands. It was quarried from bands of limestone outcropping along several of the valleys and across the rippling hills of the Hadrian's Wall area. Coal was always close at hand; drift mines were established in the early nineteenth century and they supplied ample fuel to burn the lime in specially built kilns. Some fine kilns have survived; one of the easiest and most interesting to see is at Crindledykes (NY 781672) a mile to the south of Hadrian's Wall and to the east of Vindolanda.

The effect the application of slaked lime had to the grasslands was remarkable. It was applied liberally to fields close to the farms, the 'inbye' fields used for hay or for fattening stock. The 'outbye' lands were left as rough grazing. This, followed more recently by the application of nitrogenous fertilizers, has accentuated the contrast in appearance between the inbye and outbye, rich light green giving way to dull green or olive brown.

There was a limit to the amount of innovation that the industrial and agrarian revolutions could bring to an essentially sheep-orientated community. Young working men left to find a future in new industries, and in the North East this probably meant the mines of Ashington, Blyth and Newcastle. But there was also coal in the hills, notably along the North Tyne Valley, and for a while there was local employment at the drift mines of Lewisburn (owned by the Swinburne family of Capheaton) and at Plashetts (owned by the Percys). At its height, the Lewisburn Colliery was producing 4,000 tons of coal a year, small by 'deep mine' standards but not to be dismissed lightly; the coal was transported by pack-ponies across the border at Bloody Bush and sold in Liddesdale and Newcastleton.

The extractive industries that scarred the

The remains of a lime kiln at Highgreen Manor, North Tynedale.

Pennines flourished only briefly in the Northumberland hills. At Bellingham, in the North Tyne Valley, a large ironworks sprang up in the 1830s to exploit local ore, and for a decade Hareshaw Common became a bustling and dusty hive of activity with over fifty coke ovens (supplied with coal from Hareshaw Head Colliery), twenty kilns and three blast furnaces. The iron was of a very good quality and was used for the construction of the High Level Bridge, but the transport costs were high and the Hareshaw Iron Company soon had to face competition from firms with direct rail links to industrial conurbations. In 1848 the foundry closed and Bellingham was transformed into a ghost town. The remains of some of the coke ovens, and the dam which held back the waters of the Hareshaw Burn to drive a water wheel associated with the furnaces, are still visible today on the pleasant walk from the national park car park at Bellingham (NY 840834) up to Hareshaw Linn. The spoil heaps are now covered by an attractive carpet of thyme and trefoil.

Ironically, a North Tyne rail link between the Newcastle–Carlisle line and the Border was established only a few years after the demise of the

Hareshaw Iron Company. It was called the North British line and was completed in 1862, the intention being that it would transport coal from the Plashetts mine and make a healthy profit for all concerned. This it failed to do; the mine lurched from one disaster to another and the railway survived only through amalgamation with other lines until the fateful Beeching cuts of the 1960s. The North Tyne had flattered to deceive; had the area been a little less isolated, and had there been more luck and better judgement, things might have been different.

Quarrying suffered a similar fate, though it survived until quite recently. There had long been the limited exploitation of good-quality sandstone for building purposes but it was the need for roadstone, hard and durable, that led to the opening up of major quarries earlier this century. Quartz-dolerite, the grey volcanic rock of the Whin Sill, was the ideal raw material so it was the attractive ridges of the Whin Sill that received the greatest attention. The Nine Nicks of Thirlwall, the rippling crest along which Hadrian's Wall runs north and west of Haltwhistle, were particularly vulnerable and were so severely affected that the name is no longer appropriate. The quarries at Cawfields and Walltown, the latter a massive and ugly eyesore now in the early stages of reclamation, were accepted because they brought employment and a convenient local source of stone, but important sections of the ridge and wall were removed and archaeological evidence deliberately destroyed in the process. Today, the only working quarry in the park is at Biddlestone and Harden (NT 958087), where the red whinstone (porphyrite) is extracted as roadstone for special surfacing work.

Of all the changes in land use that have affected the west Northumberland landscape, the most pervasive has also been one of the most recent. At the turn of this century the hills must have been virtually treeless, yet today this area is widely proclaimed to contain one of the most extensive man-made forests in Europe. Britain's inability to satisfy its own timber requirements in the Great War led to the establishment of the Forestry Commission and a sudden flourish of afforestation, but although there was considerable planting in Northumberland in the 1930s and 1940s it was only in the 1950s that a concerted effort was made to create a border forest comprising a series of state forests within or abutting the national park. From the mid 1950s to the late 1960s, up to 3,583 acres of

Reclamation work in progress at Walltown quarry. In the foreground is Hadrian's Wall.

Young spruce plantation
at Stonehaugh.

conifers, mainly Sitka spruce, were planted each
year, requiring a workforce of up to 150 and the
maintenance of Forestry Commission villages at
Stonehaugh and Byrness.

Wark forest is by far the largest of the Forestry
Commission holdings within the national park
boundary, accounting for 35,561 acres of poorly
drained land that would otherwise be of very low
agricultural value. The other forests are at
Redesdale, Falstone, Rothbury, Harwood, Kidland
and Chillingham; altogether, twenty per cent of the
park is made up of coniferous plantations producing
about 73,250 cubic yards (56,000 cu. m) of timber a
year, most of which is transported far out of the
national park to be pulped for low-quality paper or
newsprint. In recent years private estates and
syndicates, including the Economic Forestry Group,
have bought many large farms and transformed
better quality sheep-walks into shadowy spruce
forests. The issues raised by afforestation are
considered later in this book; of all aspects of land
use it is the most contentious in Northumberland.

The early years of this century saw another far-
reaching innovation destined to be a controversial
aspect of land use in the national park. In 1910
Winston Churchill, then Home Secretary, was
staying in Northumberland with Lord Redesdale.
Impressed by the emptiness of the moorland he
suggested that the area would make an ideal
practice camp for the Royal Artillery, and in less
than two years a large block of wilderness,
including the Featherwood estate, Windyhaugh,
Bygate Hill, Fulhope, Quickening Cote, Toft House
and Sills Burn, was purchased and turned into a

firing range with a permanent camp at Birdhopecraig.

Through the years, advances in technology brought changes in training requirements. The slit trenches at Sills created during the First World War became redundant and tanks began to roll across the moors. The maximum range for artillery shells of 4,000 yd (3,657 m) was dramatically increased and by the Second World War it was necessary to increase the War Office holding to embrace a much larger area, including what is now the main camp at Otterburn.

In the early 1950s, small outlying areas such as Grasslees, Highshaw and Holystone Common (the latter now relinquished) were acquired and by 1962 the range was reclassified as an All Arms Training Area, to be used by infantry and artillery but not by tanks. In its final manifestation, the Otterburn Training Area, used by the Air Force, Navy and by NATO troops, was extended to ninety-two square miles to become the largest training ground in Britain, making up another twenty per cent of the national park. The block of land to the south of the River Coquet is the live firing area and is closed to the general public for most of the year, whilst to the north is a 'dry training area', used for troop manoeuvres and accessible along public rights of way.

It is doubtful if many troops have the opportunity to enjoy the Northumberland countryside, but like tourists they bring local employment; up to 100 civilians owe their livelihoods to the military presence and the ranges contain thirty-one tenanted farms and 2,000 acres of economic forest plantations.

8 Hills, moors and mires

Man has battled against nature for many centuries. Clearly, the vision of the Northumberland hills as an untouched wilderness is quite wrong; virtually the whole landscape has been transformed by direct or indirect exploitation. This state of affairs is not as alarming as it sounds, however, for many of the most beautiful and interesting habitats are also the most artificial. They survive because traditional practices are still in operation, creating a countryside of sufficient distinction to warrant designation as a national park. Plants and animals that have been edged out of more intensively cultivated lowlands and heavily disturbed uplands still survive on the Border hills. Some of the habitats in which they live are extensive, others are fragmentary. Some species occur almost everywhere and are taken for granted, others are to

Windyhaugh, looking towards the Border Ridge.

be found in small or relict populations where a momentary view may have to serve as a lifetime's memory.

For many people the enduring image of Northumberland National Park is its rolling hills, and although coniferous plantations are now extensive it is still possible to find limitless grasslands created by centuries of sheep grazing. The well drained lower hill slopes of the Cheviot massif are covered by a thin blanket of soil derived from the underlying andesite, but its original fertility has been affected by leaching and the result is a slightly acidic soil colonized by grasses. The close turf is dominated by common and velvet bent, wavy hair grass and sheep's fescue, and accompanied by a few colourful flowers such as tormentil and heath bedstraw these grasses comprise a familiar community of outbye vegetation. The same 'bent-fescue' grassland is to be found in the southern half of the park where it provides the essential sheep-grazing country on better drained soils.

On higher or flatter ground in the Cheviots, and widely elsewhere if the soil is wet and very acidic, the palatable grasses are replaced by moor mat grass, *Nardus stricta*, easily recognized by its bleached appearance in the winter when the high hills become the 'white lands', poor in grazing and bereft of wildlife. The lack of grazing value in acid grasslands is emphasized still further in the areas dominated by the purple moor grass, *Molinia caerulea*. This plant occurs almost as a monoculture over extensive tracts of wet acidic ground in the south and west of the park. These places may once have been rich in nutrients derived from primeval forest, but early fertility was farmed out of them and the 'peaty-gley' soils gave rise to '*Molinia* prairies', also providing poor stock-rearing conditions. Over recent years forest plantations have replaced much of the prairie country but it is still possible to gain some impression of this impoverished habitat in parts of Haughton Common and in the rides and clearings of Wark forest to the north of Hadrian's Wall.

Alkali or base-rich grassland is rare in Northumberland. There are some outcrops of limestone in the Wall Country and the vivid greens of the associated vegetation contrast sharply with the *Molinia* or rush-dominated country that surrounds them. However, it is the Whin Sill that provides the most interesting 'sweet' grassland

Thyme, a common flower of the Whin Sill and andesite grasslands.

The male merlin is not much bigger than a missel-thrush.

community, virtually unique in that the thin soils on the dip slope of the Sill are derived from quartz-dolerite and although poor in calcium they can be rich in other nutrients if leaching is not too severe. The Whinstone flora includes thyme and common base-indicator species such as rock rose, but the speciality of the Sill is the wild chive, found in several places near Hadrian's Wall. Unfortunately, finding it in flower can prove almost impossible as sheep seem to enjoy the flower and crop the plant to a stubble.

During the summer the animal community of the open grassland is limited but interesting. Whinchats, skylarks and meadow pipits are the common passerine birds, the latter rearing its young on the larvae of grass-feeding insects such as the antler-moth and the purple click-beetle *Corymbites cupreus*, but in turn supporting a population of cuckoos and merlins. The grassland and heath of the national park maintains up to twenty-five pairs of merlins, a comparatively high figure compared with other parks but by no means encouraging. Merlins range widely during the winter but those breeding in the Cheviots hunt the grassy spurs of hill crests and nest in old crows' nests in trees rather than on the ground. Small-scale afforestation may therefore be beneficial to this rare and decreasing falcon, as it is in the case of the black grouse.

Although much of the grassland is poor in wildlife, there are enough marshes and rushy basins left to encourage waders to nest. The commonest true wading bird is the curlew whose bubbling song and display flight is such an integral part of the uplands in spring. Snipe, golden plover and, very locally, dunlin, also breed in the park, and rarities such as the dotterel occur on passage and may one day summer on the hills. Mammals have always been well represented in the Border hills. This was reputed to be the last place in England to harbour a wolf, and although it is not anticipated that this fine beast or even the lowly polecat will return to former strongholds there is some optimism for thinking that the pine marten and the wild cat will come back one day. At present the open hills are inhabited by a surprisingly high number of foxes (partly protected for hunting), badgers (with setts in shelter-belts and valleys) and stoats, which, triggered by low autumn temperatures, often assume a white coat in winter. On the most remote hilltops, at such places as

Yeavering and Kielderhead, there are flocks of wild goats, the descendants of domestic stock put out and exploited centuries ago. Numbers vary from year to year and they are so elusive in the summer that it is virtually impossible to find them, but after the rut in October they come down on to the lower hills and may be driven by hunger right into the Cheviot valleys. Goats may not be very beautiful creatures but they are a link with our own primitive beginnings as farmers of the hills, when wolves were a threat rather than a folk memory.

Fortunately for us the flora of the open hills was not entirely removed by centuries of improvement and over-grazing. Locally in the Cheviot valleys there are remnants of a more colourful grassland, studded with flowers. Alwinton in the upper Coquet Valley has the jewel of these relict species, a left-over from late or early post-glacial times called Jacob's ladder. This tall herb with deep purple flowers and fine pinnate leaves is also found in a few limestone dales in Derbyshire and Yorkshire, but nowhere else in Britain. Ghosts of the wildwood survive too. On the hill slopes at the valley-heads of the Cheviots there are forgotten swathes of wood anemone, wood cranesbill, wood sorrel, violet and primrose. The trees may be long gone but the herb-layer has remained to tell the tale.

Walking up the burnsides on the flanks of the Cheviots offers many rewarding sights of upland wildlife. Dwarf cornel is a nationally rare plant found in this area. The andesite rocks and ledges close to the burns are sometimes topped by clumps of maiden pink, hairy stonecrop and globe flower. Cushions of thyme attract the attention of the mountain bumblebee, *Bombus monticola*, and at the higher altitudes birds include the ring ouzel, close to the northern edge of its world range.

Where the steep grassland falls away into scree there are fewer plants because of the unstable conditions but ferns, including the lemon-scented mountain fern and the rare parsley fern, seem to thrive. Unfortunately the deeper hill soils of the national park have been gradually invaded by a less welcome species of fern, bracken, and this has become a nuisance both to farmers and to walkers. Bracken contains a barrage of poisons to deter grazing animals, and although in the past it was controlled by the trampling of cattle and by being cut for bedding it has been spreading for many years. Very few insects will feed on it – the brown silver-lines moth and the broom moth are the only

Jacob's ladder, one of the rarest and most beautiful of late-glacial colonists.

Male and mountain fern on the banks of the Bizzle.

two lepidoptera to be associated with the foliage – and it crowds out or stifles most herb-layer flowers except the bluebell. Walking through bracken in August is an endurance, but by way of compensation its autumn colours are an irresistible asset to the landscape.

Crags and cliffs are not a feature of the Northumberland hills, except for the extensive scarp slope of Fell Sandstone, and of the Whin Sill beneath which scree plants such as fir club-moss and parsley fern occur. Disturbance, in particular the constant but innocent pressure created by walkers, probably prevents many birds from nesting on the cliff faces. However, the few crags of the high hills and upper valleys have been recolonized in recent years by peregrines after their enforced absence through the effects of toxic pesticides. The total numbers attempting to breed are still less than for the merlin, the reverse of the national trend and an indication that it is the scarcity of suitable habitat that is the controlling factor. Each year adolescent peregrines are seen in the hills prospecting marginal or totally unsuitable sites – a great frustration to conservationists who still regard the peregrine as the touchstone to a healthy ecosystem and would like to see more pairs succeeding. The raven, which often nests close to the peregrine and is involved in spectacular aerial duels with its neighbour, receives less attention but has fared far worse locally, and only two or three pairs remain to scavenge for sheep carcasses over the moors.

At the heart of the Cheviot grasslands is the hill that gave the area its name, but it has little in

The Cheviot summit, a fist of granite covered by peat.

common with the rest of the massif. Although it is the highest at 2,676 ft (816 m), The Cheviot is composed of granite and its summit is a wide whale-backed plateau rather than a regular steep-sloped dome. Visitors who make the long ascent out of the Harthope or College Valleys are disappointed by the lack of a panoramic view when they reach the top. The thin soil of the grassy or heathy slopes changes abruptly at a 'hagg-line' to thick waterlogged peat. It may prove heavy going but The Cheviot summit represents an interesting wildlife habitat as the high rainfall and slow run-off have contributed to the establishment of high-altitude blanket-bog conditions. Cotton grass, deer sedge, cross-leaved heath and drifts of cloudberry dominate the peat summit, and the discovery in the 1970s of two rare moths, the broad-bordered white underwing and the northern dart, suggests that the lonely and unlovely plateau might repay further study and produce more relict arctic/alpine species that have survived in this limited area for thousands of years. Nearby, the base-rich valley-heads of the Henhole and the Bizzle contain contrasting plant communities of similar distinction.

Cotton grass, which survives on the wet acidic peat of the Border Mires.

At lower altitudes in the national park, weather conditions in prehistoric times of high rainfall and strong winds saw the development of blanket bogs. The block of land between the Irthing and the North Tyne once contained an interlocking mosaic of *Molinia* prairie and of mires evolved from shallow glacial lakes; although much of this area has recently been planted with coniferous trees, the fragmentary mire system that remains is of international importance and is protected within a nature reserve complex.

A scarce species nationally, the large heath butterfly is still found on most Northumberland mires.

The peat bogs that make up the 'Border Mires' depend for their continued existence on high rainfall and impeded drainage, developing a quilt of sphagnum moss over which lies a tracery of rare and beautiful flowering plants. It is impossible to guess from a distance that these 'flows' and 'flothers', often completely enclosed within plantations, are of any wildlife interest at all. They look dangerous and dull, but at close quarters the juxtaposed colours resolve themselves into a host of different sphagnum species. The series of mires varies in wetness and this influences the amount of sphagnum cover and the species composition. Haining Head Moss (NY 71–75–) is one of the wettest and richest; Coomb Rigg (NY 69–79–) lies at the other extreme, with a good deal of heather and

cotton grass. Cranberry is found on most of the mires, as is bog asphodel and round-leaved sundew. Bog rosemary, a beautiful diminutive member of the heather family otherwise known by its more attractive scientific name *Andromeda*, is a little more local but is much commoner here than in any other part of England.

Several insects are particularly associated with the mires. Of these the Manchester treble-bar moth, a rather small Geometrid found on cranberry, is regarded by entomologists as a speciality. More impressive and perhaps of greater national significance, the large heath butterfly still thrives on the Borders and over seventy colonies have been identified in a survey of Northumberland sites, of which a large proportion occur in the national park. The butterfly, which is on the wing in early July, lays its eggs on cotton grass, not on white beak-sedge as stated in most books, and there seems to be a positive correlation between its abundance and the number of tussocks of cotton sedge on a mire. The large heath has decreased alarmingly in England with the loss of upland mires and its future may well rest on the conservation of key sites such as the Irthinghead complex.

Outside the southern section of the park, expanses of blanket bog are widespread. Those in the Ministry of Defence Training Area, protected from drainage and disturbance, contain the majority of nesting sites for the dunlin, the only bird to require damp and exposed conditions to the exclusion of all other habitats. There are also some attractive and flower-rich mires on the accessible Fell Sandstone hills of Simonside and Harbottle, often merging into areas of heather.

The presence of heather is taken for granted on many a hill walk but it is absent from lime-rich soil and does badly on waterlogged ground. The podzols of well drained sandstone uplands are a different matter however, and dense carpets of heather have developed over the Fell Sandstone encircling the Cheviots. At one time heather was much more extensive on the granite at the heart of the Cheviots too, but an increase in sheep grazing at the expense of grouse management has led to a much sparser covering in this area.

The heather moors of today were greatly extended in the eighteenth and nineteenth centuries to provide better grazing for sheep and sport for wealthy landowners. The finest remaining examples of moors are those where some degree of

Bog rosemary, growing among cotton grass, sedges and cranberry, on a platform of bog moss.

management is still practised. Young heather shoots are the staple diet of red grouse, and the burning of patches of heather each year to establish a mosaic of different-aged heather ensures constant food and cover for nesting. The rotation on well managed moors is between seven and fifteen years, and although this leads to large numbers of grouse (up to 300 per square mile) it is not conducive to a varied flora and fauna. Fortunately the wide expanses of heather across the Harbottle and Simonside hills are broken by crags, cleughs and bogs, and even where the moors are heavily keepered, as on the hills between Hepple and Harwood Forest, there are plenty of secluded corners not destined to be put to the torch which provide refuge for predatory birds and animals.

Apart from grouse the intensively managed heather moors do not attract very many birds. However, curlews are numerous, meadow pipits are abundant in the breeding season, and golden plovers seem to prefer freshly burnt stretches of moor where they can nest in the open with an unimpeded view. Old heather, allowed to grow above knee height and burnt infrequently, provides the necessary sites for ground-nesting merlins

Heather burning at Midgy Ha.

which, as on the Cheviot grasslands, require a limitless supply of pipits if they are to breed successfully. Over-mature or derelict heather allows many lichens, mosses and calcifugal plants to colonize the ground as the old bushes fall apart, but in normal circumstances the dominance of heather is absolute and it is only on rocky outcrops and in wet hollows that other shrubs occur. Bell heather is

Heather moorland at Hepplewoodside.

characteristic of the dry rocky ground and cross-leaved heath sometimes assumes dominance in the hollows. Bilberry is locally abundant on the moor edge, beneath old heather cover and at higher altitudes, but it is heavily grazed by sheep and is quickly stripped of berries by birds.

During the late summer bee-keepers take their hives up to the 'black land' to plunder the rich harvest of nectar and pollen. As well as millions of hive bees, the flowering heather feeds a host of other insects, including bumblebees and wasps, flies and moths. Other habitats may be more varied and contain greater species diversity, but on heather moorland the insects are readily visible and attract attention. Hoverflies such as the large yellow and black wasp mimic, *Sericomyia silentis*, are abundant. Beetles are also numerous and the Northumberland moors harbour two nationally rare ground beetles, *Carabus glabratus* and *C. nitens*, as well as their commoner relative, the green tiger beetle.

Unlike most beetles, the tiger beetle is very active in warm sunshine and is often noticed by walkers.

Heather or bilberry are the foodplants for over fifty species of moths, many of which are large and are on the wing by day. In Northumberland these include such characteristic species as the scarce

silver 'y', glaucous shears, light knot grass, wood
tiger and clouded buff – the latter now restricted to
the Holystone Burn area. Many of the larvae of
moorland moths are very hairy and are known
collectively as wooly bears or 'oobits' by local
children (the word is derived from the Old English
'wol bode' meaning hairy worm). The vapourer,
ruby tiger, fox-moth and northern eggar all come
into this category and although heavily parasitized
they have years of great abundance. The dark
tussock is much scarcer, though widespread on the
Northumberland heather moors, and this remains a
national stronghold for the species. Perhaps the
most notable of the moorland moths is the emperor,
on the wing in May when the males can be seen
dashing over the heather in search of emerging
females. The resulting larvae, over three inches
long and bright green with black hoops, are
remarkably well camouflaged on the fresh heather
shoots in late summer. Again, parasitic infestations
(in this case mainly by Tachinid flies) cause
variations in abundance from year to year and the
colonies seem to drift across the moors following
optimum heather cover after burning, but together
with the northern eggar the emperor is the most
likely creature to make an impression on summer
picnickers.

Moorland moths:
emperor (left) and fox
moth (about two-thirds
life size).

9 **Loughs, burns and denes**

Broomlee Lough, to the north of the Whin Sill near Housesteads.

Many of the Border mires were once shallow lakes left by retreating ice. Caw Lough, north of Hadrian's Wall, is shown on early maps as open water but it is now a swamp. Thousands of years ago there must have been dozens of pools or small lakes between the North and South Tyne Rivers, but now there are only a handful contained in a few square miles around Housesteads. These lakes or loughs (pronounced 'loffs') are of considerable wildlife interest but are so small compared with the artificial reservoirs of Kielder and Catcleugh on the national park boundaries that they attract little attention and have been affected over the years by sailing and angling. Broomlee Lough (NY 79–69–) remains the least spoilt and has a rich aquatic and marginal flora, whilst Crag Lough, beneath Highshields Crags on the line of the Whin Sill, has been damaged by toxic

chemicals introduced to kill off coarse fish and thereby improve its stock of trout.

The main ecological interest in the glacial loughs lies in the sequence of open water through fen or swamp to grassland or woodland, and from the varied base quality of the water. Bird life is not especially rich in the summer, although in recent years great crested grebes have attempted to breed at Broomlee and there are always teal, shoveler and tufted ducks on the water. During the winter the situation is much more exciting and the loughs usually hold interesting wildfowl. Greenlee Lough (NY 77–69–) is noted for its flocks of goldeneye and goosander (up to 120 have been recorded) and for occasional smew. Grindon Lough (NY 80–67–) lies a little way to the south of the Whin Sill but it is easy to view from a Stanegate side-road and attracts a regular wintering herd of greylag geese and occasional parties of pink-footed, barnacle and bean geese. Whooper swans are regular and small family groups of Bewick's swans stop over on their migration to wintering grounds in Ireland. Apart from wildfowl, Grindon is noted for waders – black-tailed godwit, ruff and greenshank are regular passage migrants – and is also a good place to see wintering hen harriers.

It is tempting to imagine the Northumberland loughs in early post-glacial times when whooper swans and a host of other tundra or taiga breeding species would have summered in the area; doubtless they will nest again one day and the presence of such birds year by year is both reassuring and an uneasy reminder that the next Ice Age is due. In other parts of the national park, standing water is restricted to ponds, too small to sustain winter birds for long.

Rain that is not impeded to form loughs or mires finds its way via sikes and burns into major river valleys. None of these rivers is of any great size though the valleys, created by faulting and glaciation, are wide and contain important woods and meadows as well as road systems serving isolated communities at the heart of the national park and Border hills. The upper reaches of burns and rivers are fast flowing because of the steep gradient, and the water is clean, cold and rich in oxygen. In Northumberland the headwaters of most burns lie over sandstone, granite or weathered andesite and the water is therefore low in nutrients.

The limitations of aquatic life may seem prohibitive but in fact it is the specialization imposed

One of the largest insects of upland burns is the stonefly.

by the conditions that makes the wildlife so interesting. Pick up a submerged stone from the bed of any burn or river in the national park in early spring and turn it over; it will almost certainly be alive with strange primitive creatures with compressed slip-streamed bodies, adapted to cling fast or scuttle crab-wise over the stone's surface to find food or avoid predators. Most of these creatures are mayfly nymphs, *Ecdyonurus* and *Rhithrogena*, but the biggest (over an inch long) and by far the most impressive are the stonefly nymphs of *Perla bipunctata* and *Dinocras cephalotes*. Most mayfly nymphs have three long tails, whereas stoneflies have only two, otherwise the two insect groups look similar in their immature stages. The larger stonefly nymphs are carnivorous, take three years to mature, and live for several days as adults. Mayflies are usually herbivores, live for one or two years in the water, then emerge to spend a few hectic hours as adults.

The other semi-aquatic insect that comes readily to the attention of anyone exploring streams and ponds is the caddisfly. The larvae are well known for their habit of constructing a protective tube in which to live, but in the fastest or torrential reaches of streams this does not save them from being swept away, and the tube-builders are replaced by net-spinning caddisflies of the genus *Plectrocnemia* which live on pads of rough silk stuck to the undersides of stones. Where the burns or rivers level off to allow a substrate to form, the silt is too unstable for plants to gain a firm anchorage and most invertebrate animals still rely on algae or on fragments of food carried downstream. This is the habitat for tube-building caddisfly larvae, and is also selected by the largest of the British mayflies, *Ephemera danica*, which spends its immature life submerged in the silt. The pre-adult (dun) of this species is known to fly-fishermen as the green drake, whilst the adult male is called the black drake and the female the grey drake. When the female has deposited her eggs and is floating dead on the water she is known as the 'spent gnat'. Obviously the range of names is an indication of the importance of *Ephemera* as a food for trout and as a subject for angling mythology.

Riverine predators of aquatic insects include most fish (minnows and stone loach as well as trout) although salmon and sea trout are more interested in spawning than in feeding when they make their way upstream in spring and summer. Many birds

associated directly with upland rivers time their
breeding season to synchronize with the state of the
insect population. The dipper, which resembles a
wren in shape but is the size of a blackbird, can
often be heard singing in early January and has
young in the nest by the end of March. Dippers
collect their food underwater by diving or wading,
and early nesting capitalizes on the abundance of
aquatic insects that are full grown but have not yet
emerged from the water as adults. In the case of the
grey wagtail the start of the breeding season is a
little later so that the birds can feed their young on
adult insects picked up along the water's edge. Both
the dipper and the grey wagtail are found on all the
Northumberland rivers and burns, although the
wagtail is not so hardy and is quick to move
downstream in severe weather.

Wading birds make use of the rivers and wider
burns, nesting on shingle banks amongst the flotsam
brought down by winter floods. Oystercatchers are
the most pervasive and obtrusive of these birds;
their piping calls and bright colours are difficult to
miss. In recent years river nest-sites have been so
successful compared with more traditional coastal
sites that the population is now expanding on to

Linhope Burn.

farmland, the birds feeding on worms rather than freshwater mussels, but at the end of the summer they still move back to the coast. Most inland-nesting oystercatchers in Northumberland cross the Pennines and spend the winter in Morecambe Bay. By contrast, common sandpipers are summer visitors to Britain and spend the winter in Africa. They are not so ostentatious as oystercatchers and this leads to the impression that they are not so common or are decreasing. However, most of the rivers and burns have a pair of nesting sandpipers, sometimes every hundred yards right up to the narrowest of burns. Sandpipers are faithful to their own piece of the river, and a ringed bird is known to have returned to the same stretch of the Harthope Burn at Langleeford for seven years in succession.

Other characteristic birds of the Northumberland burns include the sand martin and the heron, but not the kingfisher which finds the winters too severe. Of the waterfowl, teal and mallard nest in large numbers, often selecting sites on the open hills some way from the burn to which they will eventually lead their brood. Undoubtedly the most impressive of the burn-nesting wildfowl, and a speciality of Northumberland, is the goosander. Until the 1950s this beautiful 'saw-bill' duck was not known to nest in England, but a pair was discovered in upper Coquetdale and since then the breeding population has increased to take in most of the rivers and burns. The male is so large and distinctive that it is difficult to believe that the species can nest in hollow trees and clefts overlooking insignificant Cheviot burns. In fact, survival dictates that the colourful male does not loaf around the nest-site to give its position away to predators, and in April, when the females are brooding eggs, the males leave the nest-sites and gather in small groups in less obvious places. In mid-May when the females take their broods on to the burns to find their first meals of minnows, most males are engaged in a moult-migration to Scotland or Norway.

Birds that feed on fish are often persecuted by anglers and bailiffs, and in Scotland the goosander is not protected as it is on this side of the Border. The same sporting interests have led to some antagonism and trouble for river mammals too; Northumberland is one of the few remaining English counties to have a healthy population of otters and until quite recently they were hunted and classed as vermin. This probably made little difference to the

Very few people are privileged to have seen a wild otter. In Northumberland otters are very shy and almost invariably nocturnal.

otter population and was not the reason for its decline in the 1950s. The slight increase in numbers following the banning of pesticides such as dieldrin was made possible because the rivers had not been cleared or 'canalized' in the meantime. In such circumstances the continuation of hunting would not have been acceptable on conservation or moral grounds. Today otters are still present along some of the larger rivers and sometimes range high into the headwaters, but they are rarely seen by anyone other than anglers and early-morning poachers.

Mink arrived on the upper reaches of the rivers in the late 1970s or early 1980s. Whether they are as damaging to riverside wildlife as has been claimed is open to question, for in stable conditions they are territorial and act as general predators in much the same way as stoats. It would have been better if mink had not arrived in the first place, but the concerted efforts of keepers and bailiffs are not effective in controlling numbers, merely destabilizing the population, and it would be wiser to accept that we have a new inhabitant of the riverbank. Mink are about the same size as ferrets – that is, much smaller than otters – and most are a deep chocolate brown in colour.

Because upland rivers are unpredictable – sometimes fierce, at other times nearly dry – few aquatic plants are able to survive and most botanic interest lies in the bank-side vegetation. Along the upper reaches of burns where the soil is acidic, marsh violet and butterwort are characteristic of the waterlogged banks. Like the sundew, more a plant of peat mires, butterwort is a carnivorous plant, trapping midges and other small insects on the

Butterwort.

The monkey flower grows on river banks and gravels.

sticky secretion covering the upper surfaces of its broad leaves. It is a perennial, more often seen in leaf than in flower, and its pale yellow/green rosette is easy to find among the darker sphagnum and moor grass. Where flushes are base-rich, grass of Parnassus is locally common, and on the main river banks the beautiful melancholy thistle and water avens make an attractive show.

To most casual visitors in June and July the plant that springs most readily to mind as an inhabitant of Cheviot hill streams is the monkey flower, its cheerful large yellow flowers bringing a fierce splash of colour to the stones and pebbles of the braided river beds and shore. In fact there are several forms of the plant along Northumberland rivers. The usual yellow variety is the common monkey flower, *Mimulus guttatus*, whilst a less numerous sterile hybrid between this plant and the blood-drop emlets, *M. luteus*, produces a red-spotted form. Along the Breamish Valley a fine copper-coloured *Mimulus* is found, this being a sterile hybrid between *M. guttatus* and *M. cupreus*. Considering the abundance and popularity of monkey flower it comes as a surprise to learn that it is not a native species at all; *M. guttatus* is a garden escape originally from California, whilst both *M. cupreus* and *M. luteus* are South American imports.

Considering the primeval importance of broad-leaved woodland and the role it has had in the history of the hills it is disappointing to see how little of this priceless asset has survived. The recent spread of conifer plantations has been at the expense of moorland rather than ancient woodland, so it is misleading to blame the cultivation of Sitka and Norway spruce for the loss of oak and elm. In truth it is several centuries since any extensive tracts of semi-natural woodland were to be found in the area of the national park, and these only lasted so long because of their importance as forests and chases for hunting.

The scarcity of woodland places a premium on the fragments that have remained, mainly in steep-sided valleys unsuitable for agricultural improvement. Of the 138 deciduous woods identified by the National Park Authority, the most important from an ecological point of view are those of the Grasslees Valley where a complex of oak/birch/alder woods still dominate a stretch of the B6341, making the drive from Elsdon to Rothbury one of the most attractive in the park. Other important oak/birch woods are found at such varied

Grass of Parnassus.

(*Opposite*) Hareshaw Linn. The wooded dene and waterfall are owned and managed by the National Park Authority.

Billsmoor Park and the Grasslees Valley, looking east.

sites as Forest Burn, below Selby's Cove south of the Simonside ridge, and at Collering Wood north of Gilsland. Communities dominated by pedunculate oak and downy birch and containing a variety of other trees – ash, alder, hazel, sycamore – are by far the most widespread type of woodland in the park, but there are a few old elm woods on the northern slopes of the Cheviots and some fine alder woods along the river valleys, including Dues Hill and Bickerton Woods on the Coquet above Holystone and Hare Law Wood in the College Valley. At the entrance to the beautiful College Valley, on the Bell above Hethpool, are the famous Collingwood oaks, planted in the last century by Admiral Collingwood in an attempt to increase the woodland cover of the Cheviots. The oaks are dwarfed and distorted by poor soil and strong winds and will never produce the intended 'navy timber' but they improve the quality of the landscape and are managed by the National Park Authority.

   Two outstanding ancient woods, easily accessible to visitors, are Hareshaw Dene near Bellingham (NY 842846) and Holystone Burn south of Harbottle (NT 950021). Hareshaw Dene, owned by the national park, is a steep-sided valley following the Hareshaw Burn up to an impressive waterfall or 'Linn'. The valley is bowered by tall oaks and ashes and is carpeted by a very rich herb layer among which may be found sanicle, wood cranesbill, giant bellflower, globe flower, and at least thirteen species of ferns. Holystone Burn Wood is more extensive and is managed as a nature reserve by the Northumberland Wildlife Trust and the Forestry Commission. It is most famous for its community of

Giant bellflower.

juniper and birch and for some fine oaks.

The deciduous woods of the national park support a rich fauna and although the insect life is affected by the abundance of the wood ant, *Formica lugubris*, insectivorous birds such as the wood warbler, redstart and pied flycatcher still find enough *Tortrix* moth larvae to rear their young successfully. Other birds of the valley woods include the green woodpecker, which thrives on ants, and the woodcock, an ethereal wading bird most often seen circling its territory in a curious 'roding flight'.

At the heads of the valleys many woods peter out into scatterings of birch and willow which provide a moor-fringe habitat suitable for tree pipits and for several scarce moths with odd-sounding names, such as the suspected and the Saxon. Isolated bushes of bird cherry, rowan, sallow and the tea-leaved willow all add to the appeal of the burn-sides but often highlight the lack of proper tree cover on the hills. Shelter belts of conifer trees, planted as protection for stock, are of some incidental importance to wildlife, offering cover for roe deer and foxes and resting or roosting sites for herons, long-eared owls and merlins. Whether they are an adequate substitute for deciduous copses and coverts is another matter.

Large-scale afforestation is generally supposed to have a calamitous effect on all wildlife but this is not necessarily the case. In their early years, spruce plantations resemble scrub or heath habitats and are alive with whinchats. The uncut tussocky grass supports a high population of field voles, and predatory birds and mammals have a heyday until vole numbers decline, whereupon the predators disperse elsewhere. This sort of eruptive behaviour is particularly characteristic of the short-eared owl; an illustration of the maverick habits of this species is the recovery of a body from the nest of a rough-legged buzzard in Scandinavia in 1984, the owl having been ringed as a nestling in Coquetdale in 1979.

Mature coniferous plantations are notoriously dark and gloomy, yet here too there are some interesting birds and mammals. In good cone years, thousands of pairs of crossbills and siskins nest and there are always large numbers of goldcrests and coal tits. Sparrowhawks have increased due to afforestation in the national park and are now commoner than kestrels – though not as easily seen! Roe deer and red squirrels are seen by most

The sparrowhawk is the commonest bird of prey in the national park.

visitors who are prepared to spend a little time along the forest rides of Byrness, Wark or Kidland. Northumberland remains one of the strongholds for the red squirrel – the grey is virtually unknown here – and there are hopes that one of its traditional predators, the pine marten, may return to old haunts. So although foreign conifers create an impoverished habitat, there are some gains to set against the obvious losses caused by the planting up of moorland.

The wild and remote uplands, whether moorland or forest, are not to everyone's taste; most overseas visitors are impressed by the greenery and neatness of the enclosed farmland and it is this vision of the English countryside that they take away with them. The long-established pattern of hedges and meadows has changed over the centuries and there has been a recent escalation of agricultural improvement which has led to national concern among conservation organizations. Hedges have been grubbed out at an alarming rate and hay meadows have disappeared. The impact of these particular changes are probably not so significant in Northumberland as they are elsewhere; in the uplands, drystone walls replace hedges and most

An old hay-tedder in a hayfield.

grassland is pasture rather than meadowland. Mammals and birds associated with traditional farmland, such as hares and partridges, are still common. However, in the inbye farmland of the main valleys, hedgerows do play an important role, acting as a reservoir for flowering herbs, songbirds and butterflies, and it is a pity that farming interests have placed so little emphasis on their maintenance. Hedges have been badly managed rather than deliberately destroyed.

Traditional hay meadows, the swathes of flower-rich grassland remembered by our parents and grandparents, were never widespread here, probably because the soils of the valleys are not as lime-rich as those in the Pennine Dales. The very best meadows, full of orchids and eyebright, cranesbill and yellow rattle, are so few in number that they can be counted individually; ten are found along the North Tyne Valley and there are seven or eight around Coquetdale. Other colourful hay meadows catch the eye in June and July but these have been subjected to improvement and are of more limited species diversity. Viewed from the main roads most inbye fields seem to be the uniform bright green of heavily fertilized grassland intended for silage. The old hay meadows that remain shine like jewels in such a setting.

10 **The national park today**

How can such a sweep of countryside,
incomparable in history and tradition, yet alive to
innovation in agriculture and other aspects of land
use, be organized and managed as a national park?
It takes more than rhetoric and lines drawn on a
map. There has to be an administrative structure
and a strength of purpose in its management. Like
most other national parks, Northumberland was
taken under the wing of its local county council after
designation in 1956. This certainly seemed a good
idea at the time and the system has prevailed. Whilst
three-quarters of the park's annual budget
(£550,000 in 1986/87) comes from central
government, the rest has to be found by the county.
This ensures a continual local involvement and has
resulted in an excellent sense of regional pride and
responsibility. However, in times of recession and
cut-back this forces a judgement of Solomon on
councillors, and Northumberland, one of the
poorest counties, has been obliged to impose strict
controls on its spending. Additional resources for
the park must be considered alongside the needs of
roads, schools, libraries and other services and
facilities. It is within such a labyrinth of political and
economic constraints that the National Park
Authority attempts to carry out its primary duty – to
conserve the landscape and provide for public
enjoyment.

Walking along a lonely path on the Border Ridge
it is difficult to understand what all the fuss is about:
conservation seems superfluous when confronted
with a wilderness. In fact, any sense of wilderness is
artificial; the park landscape is owned and farmed
and there are conflicts which need to be resolved
year by year. The fact that most people see the
national park as a beautiful and peaceful place
rather than a spiritual battlefield is a measure of its
success in reconciling divergent interests, but the
powers of the National Park Authority are limited
and most successes come through persuasion,
negotiation and compromise rather than didactic
control. It is both a strength and a weakness of the
British concept of national parks that the statutory

duties vested in their authorities – to preserve and enhance the natural beauty of the landscape and facilitate its use by visitors – are compromised by a requirement to have due regard to the needs of the local community. The authorities can be over-ruled by the national interest, and are hopelessly underfunded when major issues can only be resolved through hard cash. At its best this brings about a working relationship between the park, other conservation agencies and commercial interests, thus encouraging genuine progress and the survival of a working landscape that is not merely an open-air museum. At its worst, it allows for a steady erosion of the traditional countryside by progressive landowners and far-reaching changes in land use brought about by ephemeral perceptions of what is best for the nation.

Fortunately, many damaging forms of land use have yet to make an impression on remote Northumberland. There is little pressure for development. The National Park Authority, which carries the duties of the local planning authority, receives no more than fifty planning applications a year, a total the Peak National Park might expect to process in a fortnight. Most of these are for minor developments such as extentions to existing dwellings, but every now and then there are more serious proposals which bring the objectives of the park into sharp focus. Two applications became national issues: the first related to a proposal to drill boreholes to test whether Cheviot granite would be a suitable medium in which to store high-level nuclear waste; the second was to create a target airfield for bombing practice on the military range. Neither of these proposals was implemented, and the opposition of the National Park Authority and the mobilization of the 'green' lobby may have been instrumental in convincing the applicants that they should have second thoughts.

Another major intrusion into national parks, mineral extraction, is negligible in Northumberland. Only one roadstone quarry is still in operation, the rest having closed on economic grounds. The potential for other extractive industries is limited; coal was once mined from bell pits, shafts and drift mines to the north of Hadrian's Wall and Bellingham. There are a few small open-cast workings operating today, but the potential for such visually damaging activity in the park is clearly very limited.

Agriculture has shaped the countryside in such a

way that it is not easy to apportion merit or blame. Many farmers would claim that the beauty and diversity of the landscape is due to its continued use as an economic resource, to be controlled and adapted as necessary for maximum profitability and social benefit. Heather moorland and hay meadows support the case to a point; they are semi-natural features that would not have appeared at all had they not been artificially created and maintained. They have now served their original purpose and a good farmer would claim that the uplands would support more sheep if they were drained, re-seeded and fenced, whilst the meadows could be ploughed and turned over to silage production. However, more and more people believe that technology and agricultural innovation has advanced well beyond the needs of the country. Parts of lowland England have been transformed by 'agri-business' into a green desert, but it does not necessarily follow that the uplands should go the same way. Many upland areas are, after all, contained within national parks and conservation and the continuation of traditional farming should be important considerations. Contradictions abound in this, the central issue of land use in the uplands. If the land is not farmed it will lose its character, yet if

The North Tyne Valley, looking north west from Lanehead.

it is farmed to maximize production it will as surely
lose the beauty that led to the designation of national
parks in the first place. Grants have been paid to
farmers for agricultural improvements, yet many
'improvements' remove attractive landscape
features and reduce wildlife habitats. Subsidies are

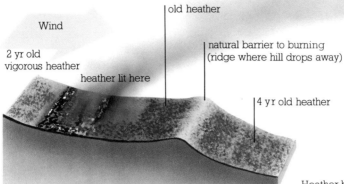

Heather burning.

paid on the number of sheep and cattle kept, yet
over grazing has already led to the creation of
monotonous expanses of mat grass, useless to stock
and wildlife alike.

The Wildlife and Countryside Acts of 1981 and
1985 have resulted in significant changes in the
conservation role of the National Park Authority.
The parks are notified of all grant-aided
improvements and can enter into voluntary
management agreements with landowners. In
almost every case the park's influence can be used
to persuade farmers to avoid environmental
damage. If a park objects to a farm improvement,
however, and is supported by ministers, a
management agreement is obligatory and
compensation has to be paid. This system has its
critics, the main defect being that landowners are
paid to do nothing. In the future we may see the
support of hill farming applied in a more positive
way, with farmers receiving payments to manage
the land more sensitively. In the case of the Cheviot
hills, for example, this might result in the adoption of
lower stocking levels with an implicit stress on
quality rather than quantity. Heather burning might
be reintroduced and mires protected rather than
drained.

To some farmers, such changes in priorities may
be difficult to come to terms with, but there is no
reason why the criteria for good farming should not

Differences in
management can bring
about surprising changes
in the appearance of hill
grazing.

Spruce trees being forested by the Forestry Commission.

advance to embrace environmental as well as economic considerations, particularly in an era of overproduction when hill subsidies are no more than social payments to maintain rural communities and their associated agricultural system. Landscape features associated with hill farms are important both on visual and nature-conservation grounds, and until a broader strategy is adopted the National Park Authority will be obliged to pick at the edges of the problem. Currently, £50,000 per year is spent on conservation, in the form of management agreements and grants to support drystone walling, the planting of hedgerow trees, woodland management and the protection of mires and traditional meadows. In such a wide open landscape as Northumberland, the importance of such features cannot be over-emphasized.

Modern trends in agriculture are imposing gradual changes on the moors of Scotland, Wales and upland England. By contrast, afforestation is rapid, uncompromising and obvious. The mountains and moorlands of the North and West, where many of the new forests are being created, are the last substantial areas of wild land in Britain. While much of this open country was deforested long ago and can only be classified as 'semi-natural', it has the appearance of wild and undisturbed country, lacking many obvious signs of human activity. John Dower defined national parks as 'extensive areas of relatively wild country' in which the 'characteristic landscape beauty would be strictly preserved'. In many ways, moorland can be considered an essential part of national park scenery, and national park authorities are required by law to record on maps the areas of moor and heath within the parks, as the basis for their policies on the management and conservation of these areas.

Moors also provide important and varied wildlife habitats, which need to be retained in sizeable units if their flora and fauna are to survive. The Nature Conservancy Council holds the view that however good coniferous forests may become as wildlife habitats in their own right, they can never compensate for the loss of the ecosystems they replace. Also, although people enjoy the recreational opportunities provided by new forests, many are critical of the visual impact of afforestation on the landscape. Some places, such as the high Cheviot hills and the Whin Sill, are appreciated for their open views and any increase in afforestation would detract from their special beauty, whilst other places, for example river valleys and lowland areas, might be improved by a patchwork of trees.

However, there is a national demand for wood products and there are profits to be made, even in the remote Northumberland hills, from large-scale afforestation. Today, the Forestry Commission owns one fifth of the national park and there are constant pressures from private companies to buy up large farms and transform them into forests. The national park is consulted by the Forestry Commission on whether grants should be paid towards planting schemes, and there is a voluntary agreement detailing areas of the national park, amounting to half the open countryside, where a 'presumption against' afforestation exists because of the likely detrimental effect on the landscape. The National Park Authority has no planning control over such proposals and in theory a landowner or forestry company could bypass any consultation procedures by foregoing the available grants. In practice, an attempt to do so would arouse a great deal of hostility, and a mixture of commonsense, hard country logic and entrepreneurial zeal has so far prevailed. However, the introduction of planning controls for such a substantial change in land use as afforestation would allow all interested parties to voice their opinions and would give a clear right of appeal to applicants if a scheme were refused.

Many farmers dislike afforestation because of the

Afforestation scheme at Gibshiel.

scale of operations; in the national park most hill farms are extensive and when they come on to the market large planting schemes are proposed. This happened at Woolaw (1986), Shipley Shiels (1986), Akeld (1981) and Hazeltonrig (1980), although in these cases the proposals were not proceeded with. Any integration of farming and forestry founders on economic grounds; farmers prefer small blocks of woodland and cannot wait the necessary forty years to see a full return on their investment. Unfortunately the physical conditions of the uplands, waterlogged and windswept, make it very difficult to create forests which are both economically viable and attractive or ecologically interesting. The Forestry Commission and private companies have made efforts to improve the appearance of their plantations by following hill contours and planting more varied species, especially broad-leaved trees, at the edges and along watercourses. However, the Forestry Commission exists to grow trees and must meet target rates of return imposed by the Treasury. There are restrictions on the proportion of forests which can be set aside for wildlife, or on management practices other than 'clear-fell' regimes. The answer might be to increase grants to allow private companies to manage woodland more sympathetically, or to modify target rates of return in key landscape areas. Without such changes it is unlikely that forestry will avoid criticism as being too expensive, too obviously artificial and too damaging to wildlife communities.

The other controversial landowner in Northumberland National Park is the Ministry of Defence, whose Otterburn military training area

'Do not touch anything. It may explode and kill you' – a simple but effective message from the Ministry of Defence.

takes up one-fifth of the national park. Although wildlife flourishes and traditional farming methods are encouraged in this area, its use for military training is incompatible with the purposes of the national park, which include recreation as well as conservation. Access for the public is severely limited; in the live firing areas all footpaths are closed for up to 300 days each year and this conflicts with the aim of the Authority to encourage the greater use of walking routes. There is also the danger of coming across unexploded bombs if you stray from the designated route – but efforts are being made to have such military flotsam removed from the dry training area.

The problems cause by the military use of the national park may intensify in the future, as overseas training areas become unavailable and weaponry becomes more sophisticated. As long as the nation needs an army there will have to be somewhere to train it, preferably in remote countryside – the sort of countryside that characterizes a national park. However, any demand for an increase in military landholding in Northumberland National Park will be resisted by the National Park Authority and the Countryside Commission on the grounds that military training should take place in less sensitive areas outside the national park. While at present the Ministry of Defence appears to have an enlightened view of landscape and wildlife conservation, and relations with the National Park Authority are good, there is no guarantee that this will continue. Who can predict with any certainty that the national interest may not one day be served by more intensive management, total exclusion and a less sympathetic public face?

The reverse problem, of too much access and over-provision of facilities, is the final paradox with which the national park is faced. In 1976 a report by the Dartington Institute warned of the escalating pressures on 'honeypot' sites by a country-orientated public. Recession and petrol-prices have made a nonsense of the original urgency of the argument but there is little doubt that the Hadrian's Wall corridor receives as many visitors as it can properly cope with and that there is a need for an overall strategy for the conservation and interpretation of the area. The confusing numbers of governmental and other agencies with an interest in the Wall and its associated forts had made any co-ordinated planning virtually impossible, but in the early 1980s the Countryside Commission attempted

Pony-trekking across North Tynedale.

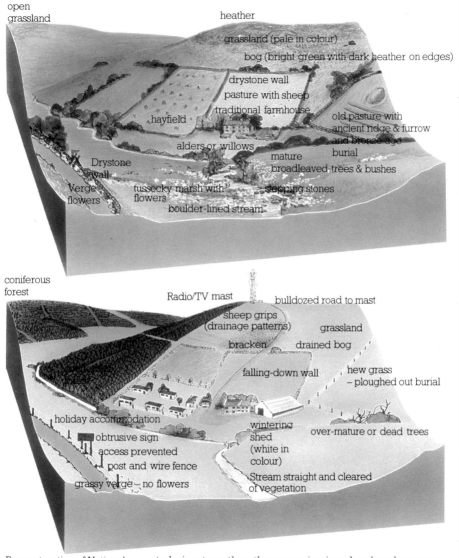

open grassland

heather

grassland (pale in colour)

bog (bright green with dark heather on edges)

drystone wall

pasture with sheep

traditional farmhouse

hayfield

old pasture with ancient ridge & furrow and bronze-age burial

alders or willows

mature broadleaved-trees & bushes

Drystone wall

Verge flowers

tussocky marsh with flowers

stepping stones

boulder-lined stream

coniferous forest

Radio/TV mast

bulldozed road to mast

sheep grips (drainage patterns)

grassland

bracken

drained bog

falling-down wall

new grass – ploughed out burial

holiday accommodation

obtrusive sign

access prevented

post and wire fence

grassy verge – no flowers

wintering shed (white in colour)

Stream straight and cleared of vegetation

over-mature or dead trees

Reconstruction of National Park landscape with and without controls.

to bring together the agencies involved and agree a series of long-term aims and objectives. The resulting strategy included the classification of sites according to their importance and constraints on their development, and the rationalization and improvement of visitor services and access. It was recommended that the central section of the Wall, which runs through the national park, should receive no further tourist development, whilst sites to the east and west (Chesters, Birdoswald, for example) should be developed to offer viable alternative attractions to the public and thereby relieve some of the pressure on the more famous sites such as Housesteads. It will be some years before the success of the Hadrian's Wall strategy can be judged; different countryside agencies have their own goals and serve their own masters, but it is encouraging to know that the previous piecemeal development of visitor services and facilities is now being co-ordinated and discussed.

People take to the Northumberland hills for a variety of reasons, ranging from a need for straightforward exercise to an unspoken desire for spiritual renewal. Organized activities such as pony-trekking, cross-country ski-ing, hang-gliding and rock climbing are catered for by specialist groups and field centres. Long-distance walking requires organization too; sixty-six miles of the Pennine Way passes through the national park, starting at Greenhead on Hadrian's Wall and ending on the Scottish border just south of Kirk Yetholm. Tired walkers want to know where they can find food and shelter. Even car-bound tourists are searching for their place in the country and are on the look-out for picnic sites, footpaths and accommodation. The National Park Authority has a visitor service section which provides information, produces interpretive displays and publications and runs a guided walks service. There are information centres, managed either by the National Park Authority (at Once Brewed near Hadrian's Wall, at Rothbury and at Ingram in the Breamish Valley) or jointly with other agencies (Tower Knowe at Kielder and Housesteads on Hadrian's Wall). There are also national park wardens, supported by a voluntary warden service, and an education service geared to the curriculum needs of schools and the adventure ethic of youth groups.

Conservation of the landscape is the primary role of the National Park Authority, but this can only be achieved if it is seen by the majority of people as a worthwhile objective. The vision and enthusiasm that characterized the early national park movement gave way to a detached complacency and it is only recently that public awareness and concern has been directed towards rural planning, the over-production of food and afforestation. The fastness of Northumberland's Border hills may seem remote and timeless; in fact the landscape is like any other beautiful thing, easy to abuse and impossible to replace.

The Pennine Way east of Greenlee.

Selected Places of Interest

ALNHAM (NT 99–10–) An old hamlet based on a fifteenth-century pele tower, now converted into a private dwelling. The nearby church is simple and very picturesque. All around are ancient field systems, hillforts, groups of huts and cairns. Excellent walking routes by Hazeltonrig and the Salter's Road.

ALWINTON (NT 9206–) A small village high in the Coquet Valley. To the south are the heather-clad Harbottle hills whilst to the north are the grassy foothills of the Cheviots; both are of easy access. Alwinton church is mostly nineteenth century but it is attractive and has a wide view of the valley. Alwinton Show, held in October, is an authentic and unspoilt shepherd's show, full of character, sports and traditions.

BELLINGHAM (NY 83–83–) Village gathered around a Norman church, once associated with a busy iron-works, small coal mines and railway, now all gone. Just north of the village is a national park car park leading through grass-covered iron workings to an attractive wooded walk up to Hareshaw Linn waterfall.

CAWFIELDS (NY 71–66–) An old quarry now fully reclaimed and landscaped into an attractive car park with a small (but deep) lake and a fine section of Whin Sill. Access to a good section of Hadrian's Wall, a milecastle and dramatic view of the vallum.

CHEVIOT (NT 90–20–) The highest hill in Northumberland at 2,676 ft (815 m), accessible from the College and Harthope Valleys. The ascent is long and the summit plateau boggy.

ELSDON (NY 93–93–) A cluster of stone-built houses grouped around a wide village green. Fourteenth-century church, pele tower and well preserved earthworks of a motte and bailey; most interesting village in park.

GRASSLEES VALLEY (NZ 95–97–) The B6341 south west of Rothbury passes through this, the most attractively wooded valley in the national park, with a walled deer park at Billsmoor and some excellent oak, birch and alder thickets

HEDGEHOPE (NT 94–19–) The most attractive of the higher Cheviot summits, though at 2,348 ft (715 m) it is slightly lower than the Cheviot itself. Accessible from the Breamish or Harthope Valleys. Excellent views.

HIGH ROCHESTER (NY 83–98–) Small hamlet, including bastle-house, in Bremenium Roman outpost fort.

HOLYSTONE (NT 95–02–) Small village lying on the west bank of the River Coquet. A forest walk leads westward, through birch, juniper and oak woodland to open moors owned by the Ministry of Defence. Archaeological features include the Five Kings stones, and there is a holy well, called the Lady's Well or St Ninian's Well, where legend has it that Paulinus baptized 3,000 Christians in a single day.

HOUSESTEADS (NU 78–68–) Dramatically sited Hadrianic fort on the crest of the Whin Sill. Nearby is a small museum and information centre. The sections of Hadrian's Wall

HOUSESTEADS (NU 78–68–) Dramatically sited Hadrianic fort on the crest of the Whin Sill. Nearby is a small museum and information centre. The sections of Hadrian's Wall to the west (Hotbank) and east (Sewingshields) provide evocative and memorable views.

INGRAM (NU 01–16–) Small village in the Breamish Valley with an old church (Norman foundations) and a National Park Information Centre. The attractive Breamish Valley has good facilities for picknicking, access land for parking and toilets.

KIRK YETHOLM (NT 82–28–) The end (or start) of the Pennine Way, just into Scotland.

LANGLEEFORD (NT 94–21–) Farm at the head of the Harthope Valley; the footpath follows a pretty burn through alder groves and leads eventually to The Cheviot.

LINHOPE SPOUT (NT 95–17–) Waterfall where the Linhope Burn cascades from a granite outcrop down to join the river Breamish. Nearest car parking is some distance away at Hartside. Footpaths from the waterfall lead to the high hills of Dunmoor, Great Standrop and Hedgehope.

LORDENSHAWS (NZ05–99–) Impressive remains of Iron Age hill-fort. Nearby, and easily accessible on open heather moorland, are Bronze Age burials, cup and ring marks and other signs of prehistoric occupation.

ONCE BREWED (NU 75–66–) National Park Information Centre close to the Steel Rigg car park and Hadrian's Wall. Along the road is the Once Brewed Youth Hostel and the Twice Brewed Inn.

ROTHBURY (NU 05–01–) Busy little market town, just outside the national park but an important centre for visitors. A National Park Information Centre stands close to the church.

SIMONSIDE (NZ 02–98–) Heather-covered sandstone ridge to the south west of Rothbury. Forestry

Commission car park allows access through forest plantation to the main ridge with fine views north to the Cheviot massif and south to Selby's Cove, over heath and forest.

STEEL RIGG (NU 75–67–) National park car park giving access to the most famous walk along Hadrian's Wall, from Peel Crag to Crag Lough, Hotbank and Housesteads. To the west is Winshields Crag, the highest point along the Whin Sill.

TARSET (NY 79–85–) The Tarset Burn has its outfall along the North Tyne between Bellingham and Kielder. Between Tarset Castle (a tower-house) and Comb there are several bastle-houses including a well-preserved example at Gatehouse.

THIRLWALL (NU 66–66–) Dramatic remains of a ruined tower-house and an excellent starting place to explore the 'Nine Nicks', a Whinstone ridge along which runs a less-heavily visited section of Hadrian's Wall.

VINDOLANDA (NU 77–66–) One of the best of the Roman forts to visit; the attractions are the excavated civilian settlements associated with the fort on Stanegate, the imaginative recreation of a short section of the Wall and the excellent museum.

WINTER'S GIBBET (NY 96–90–) South east of Elsdon on a lonely roadside close to the Battle Hill viewpoint stands a gibbet from which hangs a wooden effigy of a head – a gruesome memorial to William Winter, hanged for the murder of Margaret Crozier in 1791.

WOOLER (NT 99–28–) Small market town giving access to the beautiful Harthope Valley.

YEAVERING BELL (NY 92–29–) Famous Iron Age hillfort, the largest in the county. Nearby, on the roadside of the B6351, is the site of the Anglo-Saxon palace of King Edwin. Wild goats roam the hills.

Glossary

Bastle – small fortified farmhouse
bell – hill
byre – cowshed
cairn – pile of stones to mark a prehistoric burial site, or route
cist (kist) – prehistoric stone coffin or burial chamber
cleugh (cluff) – ravine
drove road – ancient unmetalled track for the droving of cattle or
dyke or *dike* – wall
glidders – scree; a slope of loose rocks
haugh (harf) – flat ground by a stream
hemmel – small stone single-storied building for cattle
heugh (heeuff) – hill which ends abruptly
hope – strip of better land in a narrow valley.
inbye – improved grassland close to the farm
knowe (now) – hillock; applied to lesser hills and moorland slopes
law – hill
lough (loff) – lake
march – borderland
motte & bailey – type of Norman castle, consisting of a steep-sided mound(motte), crowned with a wooden stockade (bailey)
outbye – rough pasture or moorland grazing, away from the farm
pele – originally a fortified enclosure; by sixteenth century a small square tower
quartz-dolerite – basic, coarsely grained, igneous rock
reiver – robber
shieling – custom of moving livestock to another region on a seasonal basis; also, a hut or small building used as a summer home during this seasonal cycle
sike – ditch or small burn
steading – farmhouse with farm buildings around it
stell – a circular enclosure of stone for sheltering sheep

Bibliography

Beckensall, S *Northumberland's Prehistoric Rock Carvings*, Pendulum Press, 1983
Birley, R *Vindolanda: a Roman Frontier Post on Hadrian's Wall*, Thames and Hudson, 1977
Breeze, D and Dobson, B *Hadrian's Wall*, Penguin, 1976
Bruce, J C *Handbook to the Roman Wall*, (thirteenth edition), Edited C M Daniels, Harold Hill, 1978
Charlton, B *The Story of Redesdale*, Northumberland National Park, 1986
Fraser, G M *The Steel Bonnets: The Story of the Anglo-Scottish Border Reivers*, Pan Books, 1974
Jobey, G *Field Guide to Prehistoric Northumberland*, Frank Graham, 1974
Newton, R *The Northumberland Landscape*, Hodder and Stoughton, 1972
Ramm, H G, McDowall, R W and Mercer, E *Shielings and Bastles*, HMSO, 1970
Robson, D A (editor) *The Geology of North East England*, Natural History Society of Northumberland, J B Bealls, 1980
Tomlinson, W W *A Comprehensive Guide to Northumberland* (reprint), David Books, 1985
Wainwright, A *On the Pennine Way*, Michael Joseph, 1985
White, J T *The Scottish Borders and Northumberland*, Eyre Methuen, 1973

In addition, the National Park publishes a number of field guides and walks books which may be obtained from Information Centres or the National Park office in Hexham.

Useful addresses

Council for National Parks
45 Shelton Street
London WC2H 9HJ
(Tel: 01-240 3603)

Countryside Commission
Northern Region
Warwick House
Grantham Road
Newcastle upon Tyne NE2 1QF
(Tel: Tyneside (091) 2328252)

English Heritage
Northern Region
Arnham Block
The Castle
Carlisle
Cumbria CA3 8UR
(Tel: Carlisle (0228) 31777)

Forestry Commission
Kielder Forest District
Eals Burn
Bellingham, Hexham
Northumberland NE48 2AJ
(Tel: Bellingham (0660) 20242)

Forestry Commission
Rothbury Forest District
1 Walby Hill
Rothbury, Morpeth
Northumberland NE65 7NT
(Tel: Rothbury (0669) 20569)

National Trust (Northumbria)
Scots' Gap
Morpeth
Northumberland NE61 4EG
(Tel: Scots' Gap (067074) 691)

Nature Conservancy Council
North East Region
Archbold House
Archbold Terrace
Newcastle upon Tyne NE1 1EG
(Tel: Tyneside (091) 2816316/7)

Northumberland National Park and
Countryside Department
Eastburn
South Park, Hexham
Northumberland NE46 1BS
(Tel: Hexham (0434) 605555)

Northumberland Wildlife Trust
The Hancock Museum
Barras Bridge
Newcastle upon Tyne NE2 4PT
(Tel: Tyneside (091) 2320038)

Northumbria Tourist Board
Aykley Heads
Durham DH1 5UX
(Tel: Durham (091) 384605)

Northumbrian Water Authority
Northumbria House
Regent Centre
Gosforth
Newcastle upon Tyne NE3 3PX
(Tel: Tyneside (091) 2843151)

Otterburn Military Training Area
Range Control
Otterburn
Newcastle upon Tyne NE19 1NX
(Tel: Otterburn (0830) 20241)

Royal Society for the Protection of
Birds (Northern Region)
'E' Floor
Milburn House
Dean Street
Newcastle upon Tyne NE1 1LE
(Tel: Tyneside (091) 2324148)

Index